DEADLY RUMORS

A Novel

Linda Ellen Lynch

Other books by Linda Ellen Lynch, available on Amazon.com, Kindle, other online retailers and by request/stocked in select retail locations.

Secrets on Sand Beach
Blood
Emerald Valley
What the Heart Wants
A Time to Move On

ISBN 978-1-958533-14-7
ISBN 978-1-958533-19-2
Library of Congress Control Number 2022923101

Cover design by Jody Dyer

Crippled Beagle Publishing
www.crippledbeaglepublishing.com

Printed in the UNITED STATES OF AMERICA

For family and friends who stand up for truth, refusing to engage in rumors.

CHAPTER ONE

Small towns can be notorious when it comes to circulation of rumors. Riverwood, Oregon, population below 14,000, is no exception. Rumors are considered the norm in this sleepy, picturesque, mountain town. Everyone assumes they know everything about everybody. For the most part this is true. There are exceptions when the truth is boring, does not provide a desired response or does not create the level of excitement needed. This is when embellishment, blackmail, outright lies, speculation, and murder come into play to satisfy rumor mongers and individuals willing to listen to their prattle.

Architect/construction consultant, handsome, well-built Josh Morgan, a recent widower of eleven months, and lovely widow of three years, Cynthia Jane Marsh, find themselves caught up in the rumor mill due to circumstances over which they have little or no control. Before all is said and done, the wealthy mayor, also serving as a local hospital's board chairperson, and other local gossips could find themselves embroiled in unsavory deeds of monumental proportions.

Cynthia Jane (Cindy) Marsh became friends with Josh Morgan after meeting him at the annual church rummage sale eleven months after his wife's death. Being a good Christian, Cindy is always willing to lend a helping hand to those in need. Thus, she offered to lend a hand when Josh's truck broke down at the sale. Exhausted, Josh fell into a deep sleep while riding in her truck's passenger seat before they reached his home. The local radio station broke in on regular programming to announce warnings of a severe storm with possible tornadic activity rapidly approaching the area. Unable to awaken Josh, Cindy decided to turn around and head for her closer home rather than endanger them by continuing to drive the additional ten miles to Josh's. The ferocious storm hit just as they reached Cindy's driveway. Josh woke to howling winds as Cindy parked in front of her garage. As luck would have it, they were forced to make a mad dash inside her rural home. A power outage had rendered the door inoperable and partially open, but they manage to quickly squeeze through. "That was a close call!" said Cindy, shaking water from her hair and wiping her face with her hands.

"Smart move on your part rather than risk being hurt or killed by flying debris and twisting trees swirling around outside. Sorry I went to sleep. It has been a rough and tiring week at work," remarked Josh. No sooner than they reached safety inside the garage, a strong gust of wind sent a volley of tree limbs crashing onto the driveway and yard, barely missing her truck. "Looks like I'm here for the duration of the storm," remarked Josh.

Cindy agreed and started searching for candles and a battery-powered lantern for enough light to prepare dinner. "Glad I made meatloaf yesterday, or you could end up with PB and J," she announced.

"It would not be the first time I ate them for dinner since my wife became ill," said Josh. Mentioning his deceased wife made Cindy nervous, leaving her with no idea what to say. Changing the subject, she offered so show him one of the guest rooms. "It is going to be a long night, and with what we witnessed in the driveway, there is no way I can take you back to your house until those tree limbs are removed. I suggest we have a glass of wine by lantern light in the downstairs den until supper time. It will be safer there." Josh said she had a good idea. It was difficult to see in the shadows of the den, but he could not help noticing a large, woven, wood basket filled with knitting needles sticking from balls of different colored yarn sitting on the floor in a corner of the large room. "I take it you are into knitting?" he asked.

"You could say that" she replied. "I knit booties, sweaters and blankets for the hospital nursery to distribute to those in need, with an occasional throw for elderly patients during winter months to help keep me busy." She stopped short of telling him it gave her something to do after the death of her husband. "Someday I would like to open a knitting shop in the old downtown area where I can teach classes and earn a few dollars doing something I love."

"I could help you design such a place," offered Josh.

"That would be lovely, but it is just a thought now. It could be a possibility sometime in the future," replied Cindy.

Sensing her hesitation, Josh said, "Let me know when you are ready. I would be happy to help."

She couldn't explain it, but being in the den with him made her feel uncomfortable. "What about we go up to the kitchen and make those meatloaf sandwiches while there is a lull in the storm?" she suggested.

"Sounds like a plan to me. Then, if you don't mind, I would like to go to bed. I haven't been sleeping well, and I'm tired," said Josh.

"Speaking of plans to retire, the first guestroom on the right is ready," said Cindy. "I apologize for only lukewarm water for a shower. The hot water heater is electric, and the power has been off for at least two hours. Let's hope the power company gets me back online by morning when a cup of hot coffee will hit the spot." Josh didn't let her know it wasn't the first time he missed taking a hot shower, and it wouldn't be the last. The experience was routine when his wife lay dying and he sat holding her hand instead of taking care of himself.

Sandwiches eaten, they said good night and went to their respective bedrooms. Both soon fell asleep despite the storm's fury. Josh's presence at her home did not go unnoticed late into the next morning. The storm abated, permitting county workers to clear a path barely wide enough for cars to pass on the county road. Three women in a car noticed Josh working with a chain saw to remove downed tree limbs in Cindy's yard. This observation gave rise to the rumor he spent the night and what that entails in the mind of nosy observers driving around to see storm damage. Rather than give credence to the rumors, Cindy chooses to ignore them as just one more vicious assumption aimed at naming her a woman of dubious character on this May morning.

Two weeks later Cindy decided today could be the day to bring about change to what has become her predictable life since the untimely death of her husband, Harold. How this change would come about would be anyone's guess. Since Harold's death, her life has become a routine of eating, sleeping, gardening, reading, housekeeping and sporadically attending church. In plain English, she gave up socializing for the most part, convincing herself she was content to live in relative isolation because of unfounded rumors concerning her morals as a beautiful widow. Approaching age thirty, there is no doubt Cindy is attractive. Her thick mane of light brown hair is often kept under control, pulled back from her delicate face in a ponytail. Her full lips are the kind men instinctively long to kiss, even without benefit of lip gloss. Her hourglass figure is often the topic of conversation when a gaggle of women get together for lunch and she is not present, which is frequently. She is intelligent, witty and cares about others to a fault. People, especially men, enjoy her rare company even with a hint of sadness in her eyes after losing her husband to leukemia. Theirs had been a happy marriage. Thus far, she declined to date even though offers for dinner, a movie or a long weekend at a location of her choosing had been offered by eligible single men and a couple of married men known to step out on their wives.

She and Harold had just completed the house of their dreams when the diagnosis ending his life came with little warning. Cindy found it increasingly unsettling to continue living with all the bric-a-brac and expensive artwork collected before and during their marriage. In her mind, the annual church rummage sale presented the perfect opportunity to dispose of once cherished items that now cause emotional pain by staring her in the face every waking hour. She found it hard enough to continue living with the furniture, rugs and draperies they selected together. At the same time, the sale of distressing items would allow her to share twenty-five per cent of sales with church coffers that would soon pay for needed repairs to the leaking sanctuary roof. Any additional money would be put aside to help build the future knitting shop.

Church secretary Susan Conners appeared to be genuinely delighted when Cindy chose to dispose of what Susan knows are desirable items. She gave a fleeting thought to waving the ten-dollar fee charge per table due to Cindy having lost her husband. Just as quickly, Susan changed her mind. "Cindy can afford it, so why should I give her a break when the church gets so little from sales?" Susan mumbled to herself after Cindy left the church office after paying twenty dollars for two tables. While she would never openly admit it, Susan coveted the lovely Irish glassware, English teacup sets, plates and artwork she felt sure would be included in the sale. She had seen many of those items in the Marsh home's glass front cabinets and wall shelves while attending parties prior to Harold's death. The church sale would present the perfect opportunity for her to buy them for practically nothing of their true value. To accomplish this goal, Susan also felt it would be to her benefit to start the rumor that Cindy's tables would be filled with worthless junk. She did this thinking she could purchase items she wanted before folks began to circulate to Cindy's tables and draw their own conclusions. The first hour of the sale, Cindy did not catch on to what was happening. People seemed to be avoiding her tables. This was until a member of the congregation wandered by to exclaim, "Why Cindy, you have beautiful things! Whoever said all you had was junk didn't know what they were talking about!"

"Who told you my things were junk?" inquired Cindy.

"I don't remember," lied the woman, a close friend of Susan's. "I will do my best let it be known you have lovely items." *But not until after Susan and I have purchased everything we want*, she thought as she picked up a lovely piece of sculpture and offered a price well below what the Remington bronze was worth. She almost felt pangs of guilt when Cindy agreed to her offer. It did not take more than a few seconds before deciding she was entitled to a bargain, convincing herself Cindy had snared a wealthy husband by being promiscuous and could easily afford to part with belongings after his death.

CHAPTER TWO

It was past 8:00 a.m. on a pleasant but cool May Saturday morning of the church rummage sale. The hustle and bustle surrounding sale tables being assembled in the parking lot lent a festive air. Music from several portable radios played as their owners engage in friendly competition to have their tables ready for first customers. Cindy found herself stooped beside a cardboard box filled with delicate Irish glassware wrapped in tea towels when she heard an unmistakable laugh, followed by the voice of a woman she viewed as a friend, Ellie Montgomery. She looked up to find Ellie, her arm linked with that of Josh Morgan, a man she noticed only from a distance while seated in a pew across the aisle on rare occasions she attends church. They have not been introduced because Cindy always makes a point to leave before the preacher finishes the benediction. She does this to avoid contact with members she knows, without a doubt, are responsible for unfounded rumors being spread about her. Thus, there has been little opportunity to meet any potential, single admirers, including the handsome widower approaching her tables.

They laughed and talked as they headed straight toward Cindy, with the church secretary Susan Collins hot on their heels. "Oh no!" murmured Cindy. "This is not an ideal time for me to formally meet Mr. Morgan. I should have sent flowers to his wife's funeral, at least attended calling hours or sent a sympathy card, and I didn't do any of those things." She meant to but could not face having to deal with death again when she had not fully recovered from her loss of Harold.

Harold passed away two months after being diagnosed with the deadly form of leukemia. Before then, he appeared strong and healthy. His death continues to leave Cindy reeling and tearful at unexpected times. They barely finished building the house of their dreams and were ready to start a family when he died. It took the better part of a year before she was able to function beyond doing what was necessary for survival. Even though three years had passed, Cindy was still not ready for any encounter with a man beyond expected social courtesies, let alone thoughts of a relationship with an attractive and successful man like Josh Morgan.

Indecision and the melancholy associated with loss are what brought about Cindy's decision to no longer be surrounded by so many memories shared with Harold. The announcement by Pastor Evan Albright concerning need for the church sanctuary roof repairs, and the fact there was little money in the budget for them, prompted the congregation's decision to raise needed funds by having a yard sale open to the public. This provided the perfect inspiration for Cindy to sell items she and Harold had collected, items now causing distress every time she looked at them, and at the same time, she could help bring the church out of financial troubles.

This decision did not include any thoughts of meeting such a handsome man, but here Josh stood. She had to admit he deserved a second look. It was impossible to ignore the greenest eyes she had ever seen, the thick, curly, reddish sandy hair and the intoxicating smile. From her stooped position, she guessed he stood at least six feet in height with a slim but muscular build. In fact, he stood six feet four inches tall. Her quick assessment made him look like a Greek God. She was finding it difficult to breathe but blamed it on the stooped position.

In her haste to stand, she slipped on a thick tuft of damp grass growing along the edge of the pavement next to one of her tables. This caused her to lose her balance. To keep from falling, she reached out to grasp an unsteady table, sending a set of twelve delicate, Irish, etched glasses crashing to the ground to end up in pieces.

"Whoa!" said Josh, reaching out to steady her and the table before more items followed suit to end up broken on the blacktop. "Looks like you could use a hand."

Embarrassed, Cindy unsteadily sat back on her haunches to avoid shards of broken glass while gazing up at him. "I am so sorry. I am such a klutz. Thank you for your help, but I can manage from here." In her haste to stand and put distance between Josh and her, she sent several teapots to join the glasses on the parking lot surface before fully getting to her feet. Thankfully, only one teapot ended up broken. Her actions gave Josh an opportunity to reach down to pick up the two pots that survived the fall and place them back on the sale table.

"No, I'm sorry. It looks like I've startled you and managed to cause a major disaster," said Josh. "Let me help you pick up the broken glass and teapot. I am so sorry. I will be happy to pay for the broken items."

Cindy waved him away. "That will not be necessary. This is all my fault. I lost my balance. I can pick up the pieces. Just give me a moment to wait on the church secretary Susan Collins. It looks like she has her shopping basket full of fragile things. Again, I am sorry to have you wait. Feel free to look around, but watch your step. I would feel terrible if you cut yourself on those broken shards of glass and pottery."

Josh found himself apologizing again, even though he technically had not caused the mishap beyond simply being there. "Please allow Ellie and me to pick up broken items while you wait on Susan," he offered again.

Ellie took the opportunity to formally introduce Josh. "Cindy Mercer, meet Josh Morgan." Cindy smiled weakly and offered her hand. The unexpected feeling of electricity unfolded between them as he took her hand to offer another apology for the broken items. "Pleased to meet you, Cindy."

She was able to murmur, "Same here, and I'm sorry about the accident."

"If you two will stop apologizing to each other, I'll tell you why I brought Josh over to your table, Cindy," remarked Ellie. Surveying the number of items in Susan's basket, she resisted the urge to make another comment regarding what she believed was greedy on Susan's part before continuing, "When I was passing by your tables earlier, I saw a big, black wrought iron kettle sitting in your truck bed marked for sale. When I happened to meet Josh a little while ago, he asked if I had seen one for sale. I immediately thought of you, and here we are. You haven't sold it, have you?"

"Nnn...o, it's still here," stammered Cindy, still under the spell of the attractive man. She pointed to the bed of her nearby parked truck. "It's heavy, and I didn't want to lift it twice. I figured whoever buys it can do the lifting this time." During their verbal exchange, Cindy and Ellie did not notice Josh bend down and start picking up shards of broken glass then begin carrying larger pieces over to deposit them in the kettle sitting in Cindy's truck bed. "What are you doing?"

Cindy asked sharply when it became apparent what he was doing. *I can't sell a kettle full of broken glass!* she thought.

Josh looked at her and smiled. "I want to buy the kettle, glass and all. I like to dabble in grinding down broken glass shards and making them into pieces of art, such as rings and wall hangings. How much are you asking for the kettle?"

"Thirty dollars," she replied. She could not resist playfully adding, "The broken glass is free." This comment made Josh smile even wider. "I'll take it, but I'm paying thirty-five dollars if I can leave the kettle in your truck bed until I've finished looking around at the other tables." Cindy, having regained her senses, did not relish the thought of having to deal with Josh again, but neither did she want to lose the sale. "You just made a deal," she hastily replied.

"That sounds like a better deal than Susan just paid you for all the glassware, teacups and tea pots," Ellie dryly remarked. When she did not get a response from Cindy she continued, "If you two will excuse me, I'll find a broom and dustpan so we can clean up the small glass pieces before someone gets cut. While I'm gone, you and Josh can get acquainted." Cindy felt a sense of panic as she watched Ellie walk away. She had no idea what to say beyond blurting out, "I'm sorry I didn't send flowers, attend the service or offer condolences for your wife's passing."

"No need to apologize," he replied. "We didn't have the opportunity to get to know you, but I know you lost your husband not long before Janice died. And we didn't . . . I haven't reached out to you either." He reached in his pants pocket and pulled out money to pay for the kettle, handing over the bills with a smile, causing Cindy's heart to beat faster. "Be back before you know it, and thanks for holding the kettle for me." He was on his way to become lost in the crowd before Cindy could thank him for the purchase. Stunned by her beauty, Josh made the quick decision not to wait around for her reply as Ellie approached with the broom and dustpan.

"Isn't he a hunk?" were the first words out of Ellie's mouth after Josh walked out of earshot.

"What?" said a distracted Cindy.

"Stop standing there staring in his direction and pay attention," stated Ellie in a teasing manner. "He did buy the kettle, didn't he?"

Cindy dreamily replied as a hint of a smile played across her face. "Yes, he did."

"Then why is the kettle still sitting in your truck bed?" inquired Ellie.

"He wanted to do more shopping and will pick it up on his way home," replied Cindy.

Ellie smiled. "That means you will see him again, doesn't it?"

Cindy became defensive. "Of course, I will have contact with him again. How do you expect him to get the kettle out of my truck without me being aware of him when my truck is sitting close to my tables?"

"Oh, he could have easily transferred the kettle to his truck right after he bought it. Didn't you get a good look at those muscles? He needed an excuse to see you again," she offered with a knowing look Cindy found irritating.

"That's just nonsense." replied Cindy even more defensively. "How could he drive his truck to this site with all those people and vehicles in the way?"

"If you look to your left, you will see a dark blue Ford Pickup 350 parked not more than ten feet away from your truck," she replied, pointing in the direction of Josh's truck. "With those muscles he could have easily transferred the kettle to his truck bed without thinking twice. That means he must be interested in seeing you again," Ellie insisted.

Cindy scoffed, "Ellie, you have an extremely vivid imagination! Are you forgetting Josh and I just formally met? You are out of your mind if you think he's interested in me beyond purchasing my kettle!"

Ellie was not about to give up. "He's single. You are single. It has been almost a year since his wife Janice died and three years since Harold died. We both know men do not grieve as long as women. I am not saying you need to marry the guy! Just be open to having coffee or at least have a fling with him. If you don't, I'm sure some other woman will." She failed to add, *Me included if given a chance*.

"You can't be serious! Me have a fling with Josh Morgan when I just met him?" Cindy questioned. "Not happening," she replied curtly. "In case you are unaware, I am not making any decisions to become labeled a one-night stand in addition to what the town gossips already have to say about me!"

Ellie sighed while continuing to sweep up the broken glass. "I never said you were a one-night stand. I am just saying things are different now. People have relationships that do not necessarily lead to long term commitments or marriage. Lighten up, girl. Like I just said, if you don't stake some sort of claim on him soon, you can bet there are other women who will. In fact, I am surprised this hasn't happened already in this hick town, even if it hasn't been a full year since his wife died. I get around enough to know several women who are drooling at the thought of him being available as soon as the official mourning period ends in a month."

Cindy stared at her in disbelief before responding. "It is well known smart women in this town do not have flings openly, unless they want to be categorized as sluts. And that designation, without merit I might add, has already been assigned to me, thank you very much. I am sure you are aware there are already those types of rumors being spread about me since my husband's death thanks to that gossip, Sharon Murphy! Now if you are finished trying to convince me to ruin my reputation any further, I think the church secretary has returned and wants to make more purchases!"

Taken aback by Cindy's uncharacteristic outburst, Ellie looked at her watch and declared it was time for her to go help prepare hot dogs the Ladies Aide Society were selling for lunch. "Mark my words. Josh is interested in you," she called over her shoulder. Those words were not missed by Susan, who would go running to Sharon Murphy with what she heard but not until she filled her shopping basket to the brim for the third time.

Josh Morgan and his wife Janice moved to Rockwood, Oregon, two years ago. The move became necessary when Josh was awarded the contract to design and oversee building a new three-story wing at Tri-County Memorial Hospital, which was needed due to the influx of people expected to move into the area. Living permanently in Rockwood was not part of their plan. After renting an apartment for six months, they fell in love with what they initially believed to be the friendly, small town atmosphere.

This prompted their decision to buy a house on the outskirts of town, thinking it would be the perfect place to raise a family. Having grown up in and lived in a large city until now, neither of them had any idea what they were getting themselves into by choosing to stay in a small town. Everything was going along great for the first year of the hospital expansion which would take three years. They joined the local church, became part of community activities, and enjoyed their house not far from Mirror Lake. It was not until into their second year living in the immediate Riverwood area that Josh began noticing a change in Janice. She was becoming increasingly distant, always finding a variety of excuses for them not to make love or engage in social activities with mutual friends. When she started rapidly losing weight, Josh insisted she schedule a checkup with a local doctor. When she refused, it did not take long before Josh began to hear rumors Janice was involved in an affair with a married man, so he assumed the weight loss was due to guilt. By now Josh was aware small towns were known for their rumor mills. For several months, he believed this to be the case, dismissing rumors Janice insisted were untrue, and he believed her.

This changed the day she collapsed after vomiting blood while having her hair styled at the local salon. The medical emergency forced Janice to seek treatment at the hospital emergency room, presenting the perfect venue for rumors she was bleeding due to a bungled abortion, the pregnancy being the result of the affair; so much for the reality of throwing up blood be damned! The resulting rumor also forced her alleged married lover to leave town in a big hurry. The key word being *alleged*. Her alleged lover worked as a business consultant who set up websites throughout various locations in the tri-state area. He had been meeting with Janice, a writer, to help her put together a business plan and web site promotion for teaching writing classes. Their meetings did not go unnoticed by local gossips who decided she was engaged in an affair with the man in question. It did not matter that he, for all essential purposes, maintained the appearance of a happy marriage. It did not seem to matter to the rumor mill. When his wife heard the rumors, she insisted he left town for business reasons, and stressed that they did enjoy a reasonably happy marriage. She, along with the man, insisted he was not engaged in an extramarital affair with Janice or anyone else. Their protests fell on deaf ears.

When Janice's preliminary x-rays came back indicating suspicious lumps in both breasts that could indicate stage four cancerous tumors involving lymph nodes, she freaked out. This and shadows from an MRI left little doubt cancer had also invaded her stomach, lungs and liver, the cause of her deteriorating health and the yellow cast to her eyes and skin. Skin and eye yellowing were first attributed to multiple blood transfusions during and after the initial bleeding episode, not alleged excessive drinking. Janice became more hysterical upon hearing she needed to undergo a double mastectomy, and tumor removals from the stomach, lungs, and liver, followed by chemo and radiation. Her options were all of the above or an early death. Josh could not believe it when she refused both the mastectomies and surgeries saying, "I would rather be dead than have surgery and suffer disabling effects of going through chemo when there are no guarantees I will be cured! Josh, you must face the fact I am going to die, and I want to go with dignity."

No amount of convincing by Josh or the oncologist could change her mind. This resulted in her being sent home with hospice care when it became clear, after agreeing to a second MRI (head and upper body scan) that the cancer had spread to her brain and reinforced the fact tumors found on initial scans had grown substantially in a matter of weeks. Josh was beside himself with sorrow, knowing neither he nor doctors could do anything to stop the ravages of the disease. It was too far advanced for any form of therapy to stop the deadly process. Janice was going to die. It was a matter of when, not if. Josh was a man who took his wedding vow until death we do part seriously. He did his best to give support to his wife with the help of hospice nurses, one of whom Janice believed was a friend, Ellie Montgomery.

Ellie, a registered nurse, worked part-time for hospice. In addition to working with hospice, she filled in as nursing supervisor at the local hospital when needed. Recently, she took on the job of overseeing the hospital volunteer program when the former director retired. Everyone thought of her as an angel of mercy for taking on the volunteer program. Had the facts been known, she did this to provide a means of keeping tabs on members of the community to provide ammunition for her insatiable need to add excitement to her single life by providing information to the gossip mongers. At the same time, she was very adept at side stepping any rumors aimed at her.

Hospital board members were sympathetic to Janice's condition, the exception being Board President Melvin Pendergast, a wealthy man used to things being done his way. Melvin has his pudgy fingers in a car dealership, nightclub and real estate company, in addition to buying his way onto the hospital board through what could be deemed several modest donations considering his wealth. Melvin's appearance can best be described as a squat, overweight, bug-eyed toad dressed in designer clothing; his succession to board president was accomplished through rotation protocol with a different member holding the position every two years.

"I don't see why we should cut Josh Morgan any slack," Melvin argued as soon as he called the monthly board meeting to order. "There isn't any doubt his wife is going to die. With him moping around, how is he going to do his job after she dies? I think we need to start looking for a replacement now, like my nephew, Jude Prichart. As most of you know, he's in the construction business and would be willing to give us a good price to finish this project. I say we take a vote." The call for a vote fell flat amid snickers, facial contortions and eye rolling. Members of the hospital board knew Jude was far less than an upstanding member of the community who used building shortcuts whenever he could. That is why his construction business was in eminent danger of failing.

"That nephew of yours is a loser," stated Rick Horrigan, the no-nonsense local grocery store owner. "Most everybody around here knows it. I, for one, do not want him having any part of building the new wing. Why should he profit from taking over when Josh has been and continues doing a fantastic job, even in the face of serious personal problems? There might be a possibility Josh has a few bad days now and then after his wife dies. That is to be expected."

Melvin's face turned red. He ignored Rick's comments to call, again, for a vote. Nobody voted amid more eye rolling. Thwarted, Melvin stormed out of the board room in an angry huff without asking for a motion to adjourn the meeting.

"Looks like old Melvin's got his shorts in a twist," Joe Zurella commented with a lopsided grimace. "As vice president, I declare this meeting adjourned, unless one of you have issues you want to discuss." He looked around the room at each board member, each offering no comment or urgent business, but one member was the exception.

"Melvin does have a point," commented Beulah McCloud, the lone, well-to-do female board member appointed by Melvin. He appointed her thinking she would back him up on anything he wanted and was often persuaded to donate to various hospital needs, not to mention she hosted lovely dinner parties always including Melvin and his social climbing wife, Betty.

"Beulah, why didn't you jump at the chance to respond to his motion to fire Josh and hire Jude?" questioned Rick Sanchez. Beulah's face turned three shades of scarlet, and she began to stutter. "I . . . I would have except . . ."

"That's okay, Beulah," interjected Sam Jenkins. "We all know it would not have been easy for you to second his cockeyed motion since we all know Melvin is your cousin three times removed. Doing so would cause resistance from the rest of us that could end up with bad feelings." He could have added and thought to himself, *As a known drunk, you probably no longer have enough functioning brain cells to understand what Melvin meant by calling for a vote to his proposal to fire Josh!*

"Gentlemen and lady, I think it is time we all retire to the local watering hole," announced Ben Sommers, the deli owner and peacemaker. Not known for his elegant or careful dressing, he shoved back his chair and stood to hitch up his pants that sagged dangerously close to revealing the family jewels.

Observing Ben's move to adjust his trousers, Jud Watson snickered. "You mean the saloon where real business takes place? Nothing like a cold one in the back room of the Pine Tree Saloon before coming to proper decisions about anything of significant importance," he drawled. He was just about to leave the board room when he turned back, "You ride with me Beulah. Then I'll take you home. You can pick up your car tomorrow." Jud was not making the offer out of friendship or the goodness of his heart. Considering Beulah's history, he knew she would be a danger to herself and others on the highway if allowed to drive from the saloon at what would probably be a late hour when the group broke up. He based this on knowing she had been involved in at least four auto accidents in the past six months and was more than likely driving without insurance or a valid driver's license. Why she was not in jail remained a mystery to him, beyond knowing the judge ruling in her cases was a distant family member also known to heavily imbibe from time to time.

"You got that right about making serious decisions," Beulah nervously laughed. She is a hardcore alcoholic who can hardly wait for the next drink; although she would deny having a problem any day of the week if such an outright accusation were to be made. She long ago decided to ignore town gossips who pretended she was sober when they were in her presence, and she ignored what was said behind her back. The disease robbed her of any inclination to call them out when they made fun of her. None of them encouraged her to seek professional help for fear she might take them up on their suggestions and in doing so, they would lose the chance to make fun of her.

At the time of the meeting, other board members were unaware Melvin promised his nephew the hospital contract on a silver platter after the conclusion of this meeting. They also did not know the promise made to Jude was in payment for securing required permits after the fact for Melvin's condo building project located on the nearby shore of Mirror Lake. How Jude managed to accomplish obtaining those permits, Melvin did not ask, nor did he want to know. All he cared about was selling those exclusive units and adding more money to his already considerable wealth; regulations and ethics were to be damned if he got the desired results!

CHAPTER THREE

The evening after the board meeting, Jude Prichart's jaw dropped in surprise when he opened the door marked *private* to enter his uncle's real estate sales office. Intent on learning the outcome of him being awarded the contract for completion of the hospital wing, he did not bother to knock. It was after closing hours, so he sailed past the empty secretary's desk without giving a thought to knocking, having done so numerous times in the past when asking for a few dollars to tide him over until he was paid from his last job or lacking work. This time he could hardly believe the sight meeting his eyes! "Uncle Melvin! What in the hell are you are doing?" Jude loudly demanded. "Aunt Betty would have a heart attack and kick your sorry ass to the curb in two seconds or less, and that's if she didn't murder you first!"

What was happening was obvious, and Jude made no effort to divert his eyes from what was taking place. To say Melvin and his scantily clad secretary Grace were in the heat of a compromising position on the brown leather sofa would be an understatement. The first line of sight meeting Jude's eyes was the pale naked fleshy backside of his uncle on top of Grace, trousers, and underwear down around his ankles, making animal grunting noises one would expect to hear during the mating of pigs. Despite his nephew's presence,

Melvin shuddered and squealed louder just before the bulk of his 250-pound, five-foot-eight-inch tall frame dropped onto Grace's body while he continued to pant. The sound of his nephew's voice brought Melvin to his senses, but not before he reached a climax.

Grace uttered a scream like she had been shot, immediately followed by, "Get off me! I can't breathe!" Melvin casually rolled off her to stand beside the sofa. He pulled up his underwear and pants as if what he had been doing was no big deal. A flummoxed Grace, however, tried to cover her braless breasts and private areas by holding her semi-sheer white silk blouse in front of herself. She had left her skirt draped over a chair too far away to grab, so she struggled to make a run for the nearby executive bathroom door. She was able to lean forward far enough to snatch her bra and panties where they lay partially hidden under the sofa's edge on the floor.

Jude began to snicker when he saw Grace's look of distress before she turned with her back toward him in a failed attempt to hide her nakedness below the waist, exposing her bare backside in the process. "Nice ass," he commented dryly as the frantic woman scurried across the room to slam the bathroom door.

Jude turned back to his Uncle Melvin. "What the devil were you thinking? If you wanted a piece, why did you choose that homely old bitch? She must be at least sixty! With your money and position, you could have almost any woman in this town, but your secretary? Come on, man! I'm thirty years younger than you, and I still wouldn't climb on top of that ugly old broad, even if you paid me!"

Melvin smiled and shrugged his shoulders. "What can I say? I was horny, and she was handy," he replied with a crude chuckle. "You obviously don't know what they say about older women. They don't swell, they don't tell, they don't yell, and they are grateful as hell!" That said, he reached in his pants pocket and pulled out his leather wallet. "How much will it take for you to keep your mouth shut?"

Jude stood there shaking his head while ignoring the wallet. "The hospital contract or five and a half million dollars more or slightly less should do it," he replied.

Melvin gave him a searing look. "You have to be kidding!" He continued to count the contents of his wallet. "I've got five grand and it's yours if you keep your mouth shut." He held out the wad of bills toward Jude. "Come on, take it! I know your wife and kids need things you can't possibly afford to provide. And don't stand there passing judgment on me! I know all about those romps in the hay with Raven McCloud when you were supposed to be working late, telling Mary Lou you were busy building a new horse barn on Raven's property."

Jude's face started to flush. "How would you know about that?"

"Why don't you ask Sharon Murphy?" replied Melvin with a sly grin. "In case you forgot, she knows everything going on around here, along with at least four counties each side of this one. I'm surprised she hasn't hit you up for hush money to keep your indiscretion quiet."

Jude groaned. "I should have known it was her. I assume you managed to shut her up by tossing a few extra dollars her way?"

The look on Melvin's face inferred Jude was an idiot. "Don't you ever wonder how she can afford a BMW and upkeep on that drafty old Victorian house? I pay her off to the tune of three hundred dollars a month in addition to the car and maintenance. I might add, I'm not doing it for your benefit. I'm doing it for your wife, kids, and Betty. They don't need to be subjected to the sort of gossip associated with you rolling around in a haystack out behind the barn with the likes of that woman!" Melvin failed to mention his many episodes of infidelity included Raven.

Jude was not moved by his uncle's attempted generosity using hush money. Jude knew the car and three hundred bucks a month is what kept Sharon quiet about his few and Melvin's many peccadillos. But five grand would not provide income Jude needed to keep his wife and kids happy or keep his business from going under. He needed that hospital contract to keep his head above water, or he would lose everything.

"I didn't come here for a measly five grand. I came here to collect the hospital contract you promised after the board fired Josh Morgan last night. I don't intend to settle for anything less!" declared Jude. "Had you called me with the news it was a done deal last night I wouldn't be here to walk in on your rutting session." There was no mistaking Jude was angry. "I did get the deal, didn't I?" he questioned sharply. "You know my construction business is headed for the dumper if you don't deliver. I'm sure Aunt Betty would love to have a reason to take half or more of everything you own in a divorce settlement if she were to hear about what I just witnessed. Just so you don't have any thoughts about going to my wife, she trusts me and would not believe anything you or Sharon Murphy said, nor would any of her friends. I don't think you can say the same for Betty. Does she trust you? I don't think so. She pretends she doesn't know what's been going on with your many affairs so she can continue enjoying her lavish lifestyle. That would change if she knew for sure what kind of life you are leading on the side. Coupled with a good divorce lawyer to ensure she gets at least half of everything you own, she wouldn't hesitate to dump you. Can't you see you could stand to lose a lot more if you don't deliver the contract? And don't forget I'm her favorite nephew, even if by marriage. She will believe whatever I tell her!"

"No, you didn't get the deal," replied Melvin quietly, ignoring Jude's outburst while leaning over to adjust papers on the edge of his desk. "But that could change," he quickly added. "I need a little more time to dig up dirt on a majority of board members so they can be convinced to come around to my way of thinking." His quiet manner belied the fear he was beginning to feel.

"What do you mean I didn't get the deal?" shouted Jude. "You know I was counting on that deal! Without it I'll be in the poor house by the end of next month! I'll be the laughingstock of the entire county, not to mention Mary Lou will leave me and take the kids when my business goes belly up!" By this time Jude was shaking with fury. When Melvin saw the look of unabashed hatred on his nephew's face, he moved away from the sofa to casually walk around behind his desk and sit in his office chair. Seated there he knew he could quietly open a desk drawer to retrieve the loaded gun. "Now Jude, you need to calm down. I said I would try, the key word being *try*, to get Josh fired and get the remainder of the contract awarded to you. The rest of the board members didn't go along with my proposal to let him go and hire you last night. But like I just told you, this could change by the next board meeting." By this time Melvin was sweating with a growing sense of fear for his life. He hoped his trigger finger would not be too slippery with sweat if using the gun became necessary.

Past reasoning, Jude became a man out of control and roared, "You big, dumb, fat son-of-a bitch! I don't have time to wait on the board meeting next month! You promised me the job when I took a risk getting you clearance on your condo project out at the lake. It took me some tall talking to convince county officials to issue those permits when you didn't bother to get the proper permits! You already have more money than God with your real estate business, the condo complex, car dealership and that whorehouse you call a night club! Just because you're my uncle doesn't mean I can't beat the shit out of you and ruin you in this town!" declared the angry man. Clinching his fists, he lunged around his uncle's desk to hover only inches from Melvin's face.

At six feet two and weighing two hundred muscle bound pounds, Jude could easily end his uncle's life if he had a mind to. From the look of rage on his face, combined with his body language, it became clear to Melvin such a thought was crossing his nephew's mind. Fearful for his life, Melvin shoved his chair back and pointed the gun at Jude. "Don't come any closer or I'll shoot!" He only intended to scare his nephew, but the gun went off. Jude did not even scream before he clutched his right hand over his heart. His eyes grew wide as blood began to spurt between his fingers onto the beige carpet before he slumped to the floor. One gasp was followed by a series of spastic body jerks. His arm slipped from his chest onto the floor. It did not take a doctor's expertise to know Jude was no longer among the living. Melvin sat there feeling like he was watching a bad movie. "Oh my God! What have I done? I only meant to scare him! Now what do I do? Everybody knows he and I do not have the best relationship; I only tolerate him since he is my sister's kid. Enough people in this town hate my guts! There is no way I would get a fair trial . . . Think Melvin! Damn it, think! You have got to find a way to cover this up or you will be facing life in prison at the very least!"

CHAPTER FOUR

Less than a week after being sent home in hospice care, Janice Morgan died, leaving Josh a grieving widower. Members of the church surrounded him—at first. That changed after hospice nurse Ellie Montgomery was overheard while having lunch with another nurse at the local deli. She casually suggested she thought Janice's death may have happened sooner than should have been expected, and she wondered if Josh might have slipped her extra morphine when nobody was looking. Of course, one of the town's most notorious gossips, Sharon Murphy, happened to be seated within hearing distance of their conversation.

Ellie's suspicion was broadcast as fact before afternoon tea the same day; Josh slipped his unfaithful wife a massive dose of morphine that resulted in her death. The rumor spread like wildfire. Before he knew it, Josh was approached by the sheriff, handcuffed, and hauled off to the police station. He underwent a grilling all evening and well into the wee hours of the following morning. Only after questioning workers at the job site insisting Josh was not anywhere near his home the time the coroner determined Janice died, was he allowed to return home with instructions not to leave town. His actual release from a jail cell would not happen for three additional hours after the interrogation ended. This additional time left him sitting on the edge of a jail cell bunk with his head in his hands trying to grasp what happened.

Josh worked at the hospital construction site all day when Janice died before he got the dreaded phone call that he needed to come home immediately. His presence at the site was vouched for by no fewer than six construction workers who witnessed him take the call on his cell phone, turn white and abruptly leave. Two weeks later, the grand jury declined to charge him after the coroner verified finding no evidence upon autopsy of a lethal dose of morphine in Janice's body. "The poor woman died of terminal cancer invading multiple organs," he stated forcefully. That should have been the end of rumors that Josh killed Janice. It would have been if gossips had moved on to more interesting rumors. Instead, the rumor surfaced again when Josh was seen entering Cindy Marsh's truck at the church yard sale and again at her home after the storm following the rummage sale. The following day around ten in the morning, Josh was seen working in Cindy's front yard by Sharon Murphy and two of her minions. In their evil minds, he must have spent the night, thus providing more ammunition for the rumor mill.

"Why, the poor woman is barely cold in her grave, and Josh Morgan is already hot to trot with that piece of trash Cindy Marsh," insisted Sharon Murphy at the Friday night Ladies Aide Society meeting. "Marcella Trowbridge, Audrey

Wetzel, and I saw him hop in her truck shortly after the church yard sale. We just happened to be in the area of Cindy's house on the way home and saw Josh in her truck when she pulled up to her garage just as the storms hit. He was there again the next morning." Sharon didn't mention seeing his truck towed and focused on the fact that Josh was still at Cindy's house the next morning when she and her friends drove out that way after the county road crew made a path. "We drove out there to see if anyone needed help after the storm and saw him in the front yard. That means he had to have spent the night! I would be willing to bet they were spending time together before Janice died, or he wouldn't have been at that Marsh woman's house so soon after Janice's death!" Sharon also conveniently forgot to mention Josh was outside cutting up fallen trees blocking Cindy's driveway and making it impossible for any vehicle to leave or that he gave her the finger when Sharon slowed her car so she and the two passengers could take a closer look. Sadly, the good Christian women of the church Ladies Aide Society listened intently to what Sharon had to say between sips of coffee, clicking their tongues and nodding their heads. While several women didn't believe a word Sharon was saying, not one of them spoke up to disagree, lest they become her next target.

CHAPTER FIVE

Hearing the gunshot while in the real estate office executive bathroom, Grace's hands flew to her face in fear. She knew Melvin kept a loaded gun in his desk. She didn't know which one of them fired the shot. Her first instinct was to stay put until Melvin shouted for her to come out of the bathroom. She felt she had no choice except to meet his demand, or she would lose her job if she did not comply. At age fifty-eight and a widow with no other means of support, she felt she had to comply, even if dressed only in the white cotton under panties she managed to grab from under the sofa, the bra and the white silk blouse. She quickly put on and buttoned the blouse, improperly allowing it to hang haphazardly on her bony frame, before opening the bathroom door. Seeing Jude lying on the floor, she screamed and would have fainted if Melvin had not shouted, "Damn it, Gracie! Don't you dare pass out on me! If you do, I will swear it was you who shot Jude! Now pull yourself together, and for god's sake put on your skirt, stockings, and shoes! There is a job to be done and I'm going to need your help."

When Grace just stood there in shock at the sight of Jude's body and the bloody carpet, Melvin grabbed her arm and slapped her across the face before pulling her against his chest. "I'm sorry, Gracie. I had to do something to get you to snap out of it. Come on, baby, we need to get Jude out of here and clean up the mess." By then Grace began sobbing softly. Melvin regained enough presence of mind to start speaking softly as if speaking to a child. "I didn't have a choice. It was me or him," he continued to babble. "Surely you know I didn't mean to shoot him. Jude is my nephew. I only meant to threaten him, but he was angry and coming at me with the intent to do bodily harm or even kill me! Gracie, I swear I didn't have a choice! Can't you see that? Come on baby, I need your help. You and me, we have a good thing going here. You don't want to spoil your chances of becoming a partner in my real estate firm or owning a condo at the lake, do you? When the police get involved, those possibilities will go down the drain. We will both be facing interrogation and a grand jury!" He knew with his influence such an action wasn't going to happen any time soon, so he continued. "That would mean a substantial increase in your income, and even a condo in my new complex over by Mirror Lake at no charge." At this moment he would have promised Grace anything to keep her quiet long enough for him to figure out what to do with Jude's body.

Melvin's offer of a partnership in the real estate business would mean substantial additional income. That, coupled with the offer of a free new condo, brought Grace to her senses in a big hurry. In no time flat she was dressed appropriately and ready to become an accomplice in disposing of Jude's body, along with providing an alibi of self-defense for Melvin, should it become necessary. Nine strides across the office floor found her tugging Melvin's oversized raincoat off the black wrought iron and teak coat tree standing just inside the private inner office door.

"Here," she said, whirling about expecting him to him to take it. "Take it!" she demanded when he continued to stand staring at her. "What am I supposed to do with my raincoat? It isn't raining," he asked.

"For a smart man you can't be that dumb!" replied Grace. "Wrap Jude's body in the coat then we clean up this mess and wait until dark to get the body out of here!" Melvin shook his head and sighed, "And just where are we going to get rid of a body Miss Know It All?"

His response tempted Grace to slap his face to bring him back to the task at hand. "Stop and think. What better place than dumping it into one of those deep empty footers at the hospital construction site? If my memory serves me right, concrete is scheduled to be poured there first thing tomorrow morning. In the early morning light, nobody will ever know what happened to Jude. With his poor reputation everyone will think he split when his business threatened to go belly up," replied Grace. "I will help you get the body in the trunk of your SUV, then you are on your own when it comes to dumping him into one of the footers. Anyone seeing your SUV at the building site would not think anything about you making an unscheduled inspection as a hospital board member, even at night. But if I or my car were to be seen there it would open a whole other can of worms to the gossip mill. Everyone knows I do not go out at night unless I'm working here at the office where I can be plainly seen sitting at the front office desk through the reception room window."

Melvin had no idea what he let himself in for by allowing Grace to become complicit in Jude's murder and disposal. All too soon, he would learn she was a shrewd, calculating woman possessing the brains to milk this situation for a lot more than it was worth. "Alright, we wait here until it gets dark," Melvin agreed. "Then you scout the area outside to make sure nobody is out on the street while you pretend to get in your car. Before you close the door, you can act like you forgot something, come back inside and help me carry Jude's body out to my SUV trunk. Are you sure you won't help me dump him in the footer?" pleaded Melvin.

"I am not going to the construction site and that's final!" declared Grace. "I do suggest I go for coffee using your car now, then park it behind the building near back door when I return. Doing this will make it easier to load the body without being seen. Plus, it will give me a chance to tell the coffee shop owner we will be working late. I can also tell him I'm there for only your coffee since you will continue working for a couple more hours after I leave for home."

"Does that mean you won't stay with me until we load the body?" asked Melvin pensively, giving Grace the impression he was afraid to be alone with a dead body. "I'll come back here to deliver your coffee. After that, I plan to go home until it gets dark before I return. I'm sure you are aware, with your house directly across the street from mine, your wife never misses the times I come and go when she is home and awake. If I were to be much later arriving there than the next hour, she would wonder if I was doing something illegal or shameful. I wouldn't be surprised if she came trotting over to investigate. She has before. That means I'll have to wait until her bedroom becomes dark. This will give me a signal she has gone to bed and hope she doesn't decide to come to the window to take a second look. I have no intention of becoming fodder for the rumor mill or be charged as an accomplice to murder!"

Once again, Melvin found it necessary to agree Grace was right. He was fully aware his wife made it her business to note the comings and goings of all their neighbors.

"Alright, go for coffee but make it quick. Would you also pick up a bagel with cream cheese since I'm going to miss the roast beef dinner Betty planned for us this evening?" Melvin cleared his throat before asking if he could sit at Grace's desk pretending to be typing should anyone be able to see him through the large glass window. She acted like she didn't hear what he asked.

"One black coffee and bagel with cream cheese coming up," replied Grace, who, for all essential purposes, had recovered from the sight of a dead body wrapped in a raincoat lying on the private office floor between her and Melvin. She ushered Melvin out of his office, closed the door and almost danced across her office and out the front door toward his car. She was very much aware she had Melvin by the short hairs, and she intended to make the most of it. With a feeling approaching euphoria, she got in his car. "It's about time things are going my way," she said aloud. "That fat bastard has sat behind his desk taking credit for my work far too long! While I feel some sympathy for Jude's family, I blame his wife, Mary Lou for staying with him. She had to know he was a big time looser."

CHAPTER SIX

The kitchen wall phone was ringing when Josh, weary from stress of his wife's passing and the day's work, opened the door from the garage into his house. He gave serious thought about not answering. All he could think about was heating a can of soup, eating it, drinking a glass of wine, and going to bed. Because he had disconnected the answering machine earlier, the phone continued to ring. Although he had serious thoughts about not answering, out of habit he picked up the receiver. "Hello, Josh Morgan speaking."

"Hi Josh, it's Cindy Marsh. I'm calling to find out when you would like to have the steak dinner I promised you for cleaning up fallen trees on my driveway and lawn after the storm two weeks ago."

Hearing her voice threw Josh off kilter. He was expecting to hear from the concrete company foreman with a definite time the concrete footer scheduled for early tomorrow morning at the hospital wing. Startled at hearing her voice, he said, "Hi Cindy. I am ashamed to admit I forgot about the steak dinner offer. I assumed you made the offer thinking I wouldn't take you up on it. I'm glad you didn't forget and called to remind me." He wanted to see her again. At the same time, he was at a loss how to go about it without adding to the gossip already in play involving the two of them. Since it had not been a full year, as expected in this small town, since Janice's passing, he didn't want to add to the rumor mill.

Cindy was aware that having dinner at a restaurant with Josh, even one in the next town ten miles away, could instigate additional rumors. At the same time, she felt the need to make good on her offer to treat him to dinner for his help after the storm. But having him come to her house would make them look even more guilty than when Sharon accused them of having an affair before his wife's death. It turned out she did not have to explain those feelings.

Josh noticed hesitation in her voice. "I have an idea," he offered. "Instead of me coming to your house or going to a restaurant, why don't you come to my house? I'll toss some steaks on the back yard grill. You bring a salad and dessert. That way, we won't be seen together in a restaurant, and it will give me an incentive to clean the grill and back yard."

Cindy cleared her throat without an immediate response.

"I take it you are thinking what I'm thinking?" he questioned.

"And that would be?" she said before adding, "We have both been vilified by that wicked gossip posing as a good Christian woman."

Josh gave a harsh laugh. "You don't, per chance, mean Sharon Murphy, do you?"

"The one and only, but you should make it Sharon and her three or more watchdogs," replied Cindy, trying her best to sound lighthearted. Josh did not miss the underlying sarcasm in her voice.

"What about Friday night about seven? It should be approaching dusk by then , which will make it more difficult for onlookers to spy on us. My house is located beyond a curved drive and stand of evergreen trees. The house sits in front of the patio making it difficult for prying eyes to see anyone in my back yard. I'll make room in the garage so you can pull your truck inside beside mine and I can close the door."

Cindy resisted the urge to giggle. "You make it sound like we are spies on a secret mission."

"Aren't we?" replied Josh.

"And here I thought we were just two friends having a thank you dinner," said Cindy with a sigh.

"Anywhere except here in small town, U.S.A., and that's what most people would think," he replied.

Cindy began having second thoughts again. "Are you sure you want me to come to your house? I know it has only been eleven months since Janice passed away. That leaves room for people like Sharon to think we had a . . . a connection before your wife passed away should we be seen together having an innocent meal."

"We can't give in to those people!" declared Josh. "We both have private lives. I for one, intend to live the life I choose to live, gossips be damned! Sorry, I should not have cursed. I feel strongly about bowing to people who like to think they have the right to dictate my every move and broadcast it with their added twist to anyone willing to listen! Thank goodness I've got only one more year to complete this hospital project and get back to civilization where you don't know your neighbor's name much less anything about their private lives."

Cindy's heart sank when she heard him say he would be leaving Riverwood. "Please tell me you were letting off steam when you said you were leaving. We are just getting to know one another. I thought we could become friends. I get the sense we speak the same language when it comes to small town gossips. That is why I avoid almost all social activities and choose to live like a hermit most of the time. Overall, I love the area. I was born here. The scenery is lovely. We . . . I have the home of my dreams. The lake is full of fish just waiting to be caught and cooked. If I become bored, I can always pack a suitcase and travel."

"Don't tell me you like to fish, let alone clean and cook them," said Josh with a chuckle sending shivers up her arms. "Nearby Mirror Lake is one of the major reasons Janice and I decided to make our home near there. We loved . . . I love to fish, too."

"Been dropping in a line even before Harold and I . . .," she stopped talking for a moment to regain her composure. "Ever since I have lived here and became old enough to hold a bamboo rod and bait a hook. And yes, I like to cook and eat them, but can't honestly say I enjoy cleaning them."

"I was letting off steam when I said I couldn't wait to leave Riverwood," confessed Josh. "If the truth were known, living in a New York City apartment can be depressing. I did not fully realize just how depressing it was until my wife and I moved here. I know there is a downside to everybody knowing everyone's business, but at the same time, when the chips are down, many folks in Riverwood wouldn't hesitate to give you the shirts off their backs, just like they did for us during the time Janice was sick. I still have a freezer full of throw away aluminum pan casseroles, and it has been eleven months since her passing," He didn't mention how many of those same people cut him little or no slack once rumors began to fly that he overdosed Janice on morphine. He forgave them, but he would not forget. "Of course, there are exceptions, but I would wager they are few. It isn't like that in a big city. Many people living there would rather step over your body than stop to render aid or call 911 for help. So, I think I will eventually get used to the rumor mill while continuing to live in Riverwood, at least as a place to come home to when I've finished a project."

Cindy, being the target of so many untrue ugly rumors before and since Harold's death, needed to think fast for a reply. "You are right deciding to live here. Just be aware it will take some getting used to, or you will find yourself sequestered behind closed doors with the drapes closed. When venturing out in public, you must watch what you say and who you are seen saying it to or be willing to put up with rumors sure to follow." She could have added more examples but decided saying more could produce the opposite, desired effect of getting him to stay in Riverwood on a permanent basis.

"Is this why the drapes were closed when we came into your house the evening of the storm following the church rummage sale, or why you are the first one out the door after church services on the rare occasions you attend church?" he asked.

Even though his voice was kind, what he said upset Cindy. "I didn't realize you were closely scrutinizing my moves or the interior of my house," she exclaimed more forcefully than necessary.

"Sorry, I didn't mean to offend you. How was I supposed not to notice in every room where I went, the drapes were drawn? And did you really expect me not to take notice of an attractive woman sitting alone in the same back church pew across the aisle from the one where I sit; the woman who literally sprints out the door before the benediction and last notes of the organ fade away?" responded Josh.

"I . . . I didn't think anyone noticed me entering or leaving church," sputtered Cindy. "After being blindsided by Sharon Murphy and her fellow gossips numerous times, insisting I join them for lunch at the deli after Harold died, I made the mistake of joining them after church services one Sunday about a year ago. I could hardly believe my ears the way they tore apart most of the ladies who were not present, along with a few men. I felt like I was among of a pride of lions ripping a carcass apart instead of eating my chicken salad! That was the first and only time I joined them. According to rumors, I am positive my absences have made some very interesting conversations when they get together when I repeatedly declined to join them again. As for the drawn drapes, all I can say is the night has eyes ever since Harold died— add that the daytime also has eyes. Have you ever looked out your window to see someone staring back at you separated by a thin glass windowpane or screen? I have, and it's not a pleasant surprise. Have you ever experienced carloads of men hoot and holler as they drive past or stop at your property shouting what they want to do to you, and what they want you to do to them while minding your own business? And then hear via the grapevine that you took part in the lude behavior those men suggested? Well, I have, and I can attest to the fact it is not a good feeling!"

"I'm so sorry!" exclaimed Josh. "I had no idea. I hope you called the sheriff to report those episodes."

Cindy wore a withering look. "You must be kidding about calling the sheriff. One of his deputies is among those who have been peeking in the windows. Not only did he peek in, but he had the audacity to knock on the front door and ask to come inside for, and I quote, "for a little drink or two and some fun in the bedroom!" When I said no and told him to leave, he told me I needed to be careful when driving around town or he would be waiting to give me a ticket. Now you know, so be forewarned this is only some what will happen if word gets out, we . . . if we are seen in the company of one another, even for a friendly cup of coffee or meal."

Cindy found herself approaching tears remembering the incident with the deputy and carloads of men pausing in front of her house when working in her yard or seated on the patio minding her own business. She took a deep breath searching her mind for a way to change the subject. "Let's move on with something more pleasant, like what's your favorite dessert?" This was the only thing she could think of to say.

"I am going to take that inquiry about my favorite dessert as a yes, you will come to my house for dinner on Friday night," replied Josh.

"You can assume that is correct, but only if you tell me what dessert should be," she responded.

"Chocolate cake," was his immediate answer.

"See you Friday evening at seven. Good night, Mr. Morgan."

Good night, Ms. Marsh."

Cindy gave in to scalding tears after the call ended. "Oh, Harold! Why did you have to die? Things were going so well for us," she sobbed. "Please do not think I'm going to forget you, but I am so miserable and lonely. Josh appears to be a good man. Please don't think badly about me for wanting someone like him in my life."

Josh could only hope he did the right thing inviting Cindy to come to his home as he prepared his microwave dinner. He, too, was feeling lonely after a happy marriage with Janice. He also knew this was an area expecting widows or widowers to wait a full year after the death of a spouse before seeking another relationship.

Cindy could only hope she was doing the right thing by agreeing to have dinner at his home as she placed leftovers in the microwave for her evening meal, most of which went to the compost pile due to the food's lack of appeal coupled with anxiety.

Without either one knowing what the other was thinking, they both felt like teenagers about to sneak out of the house to meet the person of their dreams. At the same time, both were keenly aware there would be consequences if they were seen together, something neither of them wanted to face.

CHAPTER SEVEN

The desk phone rang in Melvin's office late the night of Jude's murder. The sound jangled his nerves. Rather than continuing to ignore it, he answered with the line he thought was funny, "Hello. This is the one and only Melvin Pendergast, the real estate blast. What can I sell you today?"

Very funny," said his wife Betty, sarcastically. "Isn't it time you thought up something more professional when answering the office phone? By the way, why in the hell are you still in the office? It is almost nine o'clock! I thought you would be home before the roast beef I prepared for our dinner became a burnt offering, and don't you dare tell me you are working on the deal of the century. And is your secretary still there? I don't see any lights on at her house . . . wait a minute . . . she's pulling into her driveway." Melvin listened, wondering how Betty could talk nonstop without pausing to take a breath. The news Grace was driving into her driveway felt to Melvin like being hit with a fly ball to the chest. He was expecting her return to the office any minute to help move Jude's body to his SUV trunk.

"I thought Grace was going straight home after delivering my coffee and bagel since I am stuck here winding up a very good deal. She must have gone to the diner for dinner after delivering my coffee. That explains why she is a little later than usual," offered Melvin, fidgeting with the buttons of his shirt to avert looking where Jude's body lay on the floor.

"Well, I do not see why you are working late if Grace isn't needed to type up a contract," whined Betty.

Melvin began to mumble something to the effect, "I'm still here waiting to meet with a client from out of town who wants to look at the new condo development at Mirror Lake. This is the only chance he has in his schedule to inspect the property. Grace can type the contract first thing in the morning, unless the client wants it done tonight. If that is the case, I can call her to return to the office." He added this statement in case it became necessary to call Grace to return to help him move Jude's body, and Betty would not find it unusual she left her home at such a late hour.

"You expect me to believe that?" replied Betty hotly. "Who in their right mind wants to see a condo at this hour? The streets in town have been rolled up for the night and it will be dark out there at the lake. You better not be shacked up with some bimbo you met over at the nightclub! You haul your sorry butt home right now or there will be hell to pay!"

"But . . . but Betty," he stuttered. "This guy is flying in via private plane and landing at Joe's landing strip. I've already alerted Joe to turn on the lights. This guy wants to rent not one, but ten units for a month for him and his buddies to go fishing at the lake. If they like the place, he thinks at least several of them will end up buying a condo for vacation homes. Money from rentals alone will buy the new fur coat you saw in Portland and have been drooling over. Just think, you will be the envy of every woman when we attend church." Melvin surprised himself at the lie so easily rolling from his lips. He didn't give a thought about lying to someone about to purchase a home or business not quite up to snuff. But lying to Betty? That was something he decided not to do beyond omitting details involving certain activities with the opposite sex when he was supposedly working late.

"Well, in that case, I'll leave your dinner in the refrigerator," replied Betty. "You can warm it up in the microwave when you get home. I'm going to take a nice warm bath and go to bed, but if you are in the mood, you can wake me." That said, she hung up without saying goodbye. Betty was keenly aware Melvin was seldom in the mood for sex anymore, at least not with her. But it was her choice to look the other way, and she did want that fur coat in addition to living a lavish lifestyle.

All Melvin could think about was how to get out of buying Betty the expensive fur coat. It wasn't like he couldn't afford it. By his nature, he disliked spending money unless there was a significant return for his benefit. His second thought was, *What in the hell is Gracie doing at home? I thought she was going to come back to the office to help me move Jude's body into the trunk of my SUV when it got dark.* He looked at his expensive watch to note it was now almost ten o'clock. He shoved the last bite of the now dried-out bagel into his mouth, wiped the crumbs off his lips and shirt with the back of his hand, then went to relieve himself in the executive washroom. He kept telling himself Gracie would be there to help him by the time he flicked last drops of urine off his penis, washed his hands and returned to the office. When that did not happen by midnight, he knew it would be up to him to move the body.

"Damn you Gracie," he mumbled under his breath while dragging Jude's body out the back door toward his SUV. Sweat was rolling off his florid face by the time he slammed the trunk lid shut, hopped in the driver's seat and took off in the direction of the hospital construction site. "I need to slow down," he cautioned himself. "I don't want that local yocal night shift cop doing his civic duty giving me a ticket instead of checking downtown store doorknobs to make sure they are locked."

Melvin made a choice to park beside the curb in the shadow of a large maple tree instead of in the open, unpaved hospital parking lot. Streetlights at the end of the street lent a soft yellow glow less revealing through dense maple leaves than glaring white night lights meant to discourage theft of construction materials in the hospital parking area. He figured his dark blue SUV would be less visible there when he got out to scout around just in case someone decided to walk their dog, take a stroll or sneak off to do whatever people do in the dark of night when they think they will not be seen. Deciding the coast was clear, he got out of the vehicle, softly closing the door while pushing the key fob to snap open the trunk. With great difficulty he managed to drag the body of his nephew out onto the curb. He thought he was going to vomit when the raincoat slipped off Jude's face to reveal the open mouth and glassy vacant stare in his nephew's sightless eyes. "Pull yourself together," he whispered. "It's only twenty or thirty feet to the closest footer." The estimated distance turned out to be more like fifty feet due to the curb and mound of dirt and gravel left to fill in around the footer after the concrete was poured. By the time Melvin rolled Jude's corpse into the six feet deep gaping hole he was covered in sweat and odor. The lingering smell of having had sex with Grace added to the stench. Although exhausted, he scanned the area again. Finding it empty of people, he decided to toss eight concrete blocks in the footer meant to be underpinnings of steps, expecting them to cover Jude's body. He grimaced when he heard the unmistakable crunch of flesh and bones as each one landed on the target. There was enough light for him to congratulate himself on what he believed to be the perfect cover of the body. "Time to go home," he muttered. "But first I need to stop at the office and take a shower. Betty would never believe I smell this bad by taking a client on a condo tour."

In his zeal to leave the area, Melvin failed to notice a figure wearing dark clothing huddled in the doorway shadows of a building located across the street.

CHAPTER EIGHT

Cindy felt as though wings of a thousand butterflies were fluttering around in her stomach as she backed her truck out of the garage onto the driveway leading onto the county road. She glanced toward the basket containing a garden salad, double layer chocolate cake and bottle of red wine to make sure the contents had not shifted as a result of the bounce created by a deep rut between her gravel driveway and black topped road. "I've got to have someone come out here and fix that rut one of these days," she muttered. She hauled buckets of dirt taken from around the edge of the garden several times only to have it wash away every time it rained. "Maybe Josh will know who to call. I must remember to ask him." The thought of spending an entire evening alone with him sent shivers up the back of her neck and places where Cindy had not felt much of anything in a long time. "Keep in mind this is only a friendly thank you dinner," she cautioned herself. "You don't know how Josh feels about you. You also need to keep in mind it hasn't been quite a year since Janice died and he's probably still mourning."

As a precaution to not being seen, she drove past Josh's driveway around the rural county road square enclosing a corn field. Not seeing headlights in any direction, she was satisfied there was no other traffic before completing the square and pulling into Josh's curved lane. The figure of Josh leaning against a wood frame around the open garage door of the attached garage met her eyes. The sight of him elicited even more goosebumps when he motioned her to pull inside beside his truck. The automatic garage door closing left only a dim glow coming from the closing mechanism before Josh snapped on an overhead light. He opened her truck door before she had the chance.

"I was beginning to wonder if you were coming. It's almost seven-thirty," he said with a smile.

"Forgive me for being late. I felt I needed to circle the cornfield square to make sure there was no traffic," offered Cindy.

"You are forgiven, but only if there's chocolate cake in that basket," Josh commented with a heartwarming yet devilish look and twinkle in his green eyes.

"Not only is there chocolate cake, but you will also find a salad made from what will probably be almost the last vegetables grown in my garden this year. I took the liberty of adding a bottle of red wine to go with the steaks. Nothing tastes as good as the almost last vegetables of the season before first frost," she repeated nervously. "Sometime within the next two weeks frost will hit making everything growing in the garden history for another year."

"Looks like you thought of everything," commented Josh. "Here, let me take the basket. It must be heavy. Be careful walking through this landmine of a garage into the house. Cleaning out here hasn't been at the top of my list of things to do these past few months. Please do not check corners when we get inside either. I'm not much of a housekeeper."

"I didn't come to inspect the garage or your house. I came to enjoy a thank you dinner with a friend," she replied. While not expecting everything to be in perfect condition, him being a widower, she was stunned at the jumble of dusty furniture placed at odd angles throughout the large living room.

"Sorry about the interior design," he offered. "I haven't gotten around to placing furniture where it should go. I moved everything where you see it now to make room for Janice's Hospice bed and equipment. I haven't been motivated to move things back where she had arranged them," he explained apologetically.

"Don't apologize. It took me almost two years before I could even begin to . . . I'm sorry I don't mean to get all teary eyed. I know what you are going through, not that anyone knows what anyone else is going through when they lose a partner," offered Cindy.

Josh handed her a tissue from the box sitting on one of the tables when he wanted to take her in his arms and tell her everything was going to be alright. He knew doing so would not be a wise move this early in their budding relationship. Instead, he motioned her to follow him into the kitchen. "At least you will find a clear path in the kitchen. This is where I live most of the time when I'm home. I'll grab the steaks from the refrigerator, then we can go out onto the patio." He wanted to add he would like to sleep in the kitchen, but there wasn't room for a bed. He couldn't face the thought of sleeping in the bed shared with Janice or one of the guest rooms, so he slept on the enclosed unheated side porch sofa. This continued even after fall weather started to turn cooler after sundown. "You grab a couple of wine glasses from over there on the counter, then we can escape to the back patio. Everything else we need is already out there."

The evening progressed better than expected, although there were lapses in conversation. The steaks were cooked a juicy medium rare, crusty and well-seasoned outside, just the way Cindy liked them. The garden salad was delightfully fresh and crunchy. It pleased her when Josh took a second helping of salad followed by two slices of chocolate cake, after losing no time eating his steak. To end an uncomfortable silence, Cindy offered to help rearrange the living room furniture. To her surprise, Josh took her up on the offer. The bottle of wine consumed; she declined his offer to make coffee rather than linger outside in the cool air. Josh leaned back on the picnic bench across from her and groaned. "I'm as full as a tick on a dog's back right now. How about we rearrange furniture tomorrow?"

"No time like the present, but tomorrow sounds like a better idea," she responded. As someone who seldom imbibed in wine, she was feeling warm from the two glasses she had consumed. "Let's go back inside so I can take a quick look around and give some thought to where things should go before it is time for me to leave."

"Sounds like a good plan to me," said Josh. "Give me a couple of minutes to make sure the coals are out in the grill, but feel free to go on inside. By the way, how about leaving a piece or two of that delicious chocolate cake?"

"You got it," said Cindy over her shoulder. "Hand me the cake, my salad bowl and basket. I'll snoop around in the pantry and find a plate and some plastic wrap."

Josh hesitated. He did not want her to see the practically bare pantry shelves, not having gone to the grocery store to buy more than bread, coffee, canned soups, or peanut butter since Janice died. He took the steaks for tonight's dinner out of the freezer with the hope they didn't suffer effects from freezer burn. In fact, he hated to admit he didn't know if there was plastic wrap in the pantry. He told her to leave what was left of the cake on the kitchen table in the cake safe in which she brought it. "Leave the cake in the cake safe. That will keep it fresh. We can eat it tomorrow when you come back to help with arranging the furniture," he called out to her.

Cindy agreed. "What time tomorrow?" she asked.

He thought for a minute before answering. "Will ten in the morning fit your schedule? I need to stop by the construction site to make sure the footers are ready and supervise the concrete pour and backfill tomorrow morning. That should not take more than an hour or so at the most. Then I can swing by the deli and pick up turkey sandwiches, slaw, and chips to go with the cake for lunch. What would you like on your sandwich?"

"Mustard and mayo please, along with sliced tomatoes and dill pickles," she responded. "I'll bring something to drink. Do you like sweet tea?" Tea was not what Josh had in mind. He was thinking more along the line of white wine to help him overcome jitters of being alone with Cindy again.

"Sweet tea will be just fine," he replied. At the same time, Josh could not help thinking it was nice Cindy liked the same kinds of sandwich additions he liked. It would be less of a problem to figure out which sandwich was which when it came time to eat. He was still daydreaming when Cindy offered her hand and said good night. When she did not expect a kiss, Josh felt relief. It was going to be a long night without having to relive such an experience while trying to sleep.

"This has been a lovely evening. I hope we can do a cookout again, but next time with fish caught at the lake," she said.

"I was thinking along the lines of doing some fishing over at the lake next week. Would you care to join me on Thursday afternoon about three p.m.?" he asked. "I can bring the Coleman stove, a skillet, some flour, butter, salt and pepper in case we catch anything edible."

"I'll catch them, you clean them. I'll fry them and bring some potato salad and baked beans in case we don't catch anything but water grasses and weeds," Cindy replied with a grin. Since tourist season was over and it was a weekday afternoon, she felt safe from prying eyes going to the lake where they would not be seen by locals at that time of day. Most people would still be working, older folks napping, kids would still be in school. Stay at home wives would be gossiping over backyard fences, playing bridge, or at least thinking about what to prepare when husbands and kids came home expecting dinner.

"You have a deal," said Josh. "Are you alright to drive?" She assured him enough time had passed after drinking wine and that she was sober. "Good night, Cindy. Sleep well." He stood with the garage door open until he could no longer see taillights of her truck before lowering the door and entering the house. "This is going to be a long night," he said into the empty living room.

The alarm clock went off at six a.m. eliciting a groan from Josh. He felt groggy and would have liked an extra ten minutes to sleep but did not push the snooze button. Out of habit he rubbed his eyes from lack of deep sleep. Thoughts crossed his mind of not going to the construction site, but his strong work ethic took over. Forcing himself to get out of bed, he took a cold shower and dressed, then headed to the kitchen. Resisting an urge to eat a piece of chocolate cake sitting on the counter, he drank two cups of instant black coffee and ate a slice of peanut butter toast. Rinsing the plate, knife, and cup before placing them in the dishwasher, he walked through the living room, unlocked the side door and maneuvered his way across the cluttered concrete garage floor. As Josh climbed into his truck and headed for town, thoughts of spending more time with Cindy roamed around in his head.

He parked on the street next to the construction site when his cell phone began to ring. Initially ignoring the sound, hoping the caller would leave a message, he put the truck in park then turned off the ignition. He got out of the truck, scanned the site and wondered why there wasn't a concrete truck and were no workers on site. The phone rang again, showing the same number of the caller who didn't leave a voicemail. This made him think the call was important, so he answered. "This is Josh Morgan."

"Glad I caught you, Josh. This is Stuart Grady over at the concrete plant. Hate to tell you, but we can't do the footer pour today. I called your foreman last night to let him know the Chinese ordered all the concrete materials we needed for their alleged new fertilizer plant. The powers that be in Washington informed us they come first before any local projects. Sorry about that, but we can't do the pour until Friday, and that date is with crossed fingers. I should have called earlier, but I didn't get word until late last night. I was all set to make a follow up call to you early this morning, then I got busy arguing with the government guy in hopes of persuading him we needed those concrete materials for the hospital wing just as bad as the Chinese. I'm sorry about the missed communication between us."

Josh grimaced and sighed. "I'm sorry, too. I was hoping to get this phase of the project off the ground today with some steel plates set in the process for metal framework to be in the air by the end of the week after the concrete set. This is going to put me behind schedule. To top it off, I've heard rumors the hospital board chairman, Melvin Prendergast, voiced thoughts about firing me so his nephew Jude Prichart can take over the project. This delay is going to give him ammunition he needs to make that happen."

Stuart snorted before uttering several swear words. "I wouldn't worry about those rumors. I heard rumors the other board members cut him off at the knees. When it became clear he wasn't going to get a second to his motion for a vote, he stormed off like a bastard who was used to getting what he wants. Everybody around this area knows Jude is a loser. I wouldn't hire Jude to build a chicken coop, let alone a hospital wing! From what I've heard and seen of his work, everybody on the board of directors, except Pendergast, thinks you are doing a fantastic job. If pinned down, I believe Melvin also thinks you are doing a good job, too. I am also sure his nephew must have something major on him to make Melvin try to get you fired so he can finish the job. In case you don't happen to know, Melvin is, let's just say Melvin looks out for Melvin whenever he can."

"Thanks for the support and warning, Stuart. See you early Friday morning unless I hear otherwise," said Josh. Opening his truck door, he noticed a faint odor in the air. Thinking it could be a dead animal he looked around but didn't see anything out of the ordinary until he spied the missing cement blocks. "Damn! Looks like somebody made off with those cement blocks to be used for step underpinnings into the lobby. Guess I'll have to write them off to shrinkage and order more when I've been trying to save every penny without shortcuts," he mumbled under his breath. He missed drag marks in the mound of dirt meant to be used as fill after the concrete pour into the footers. He then spotted a man wearing a nondescript, dark-colored t-shirt, worn jeans and dirty tennis shoes, a man who stood waving his arms and shouting frantically trying to attract attention from across the street.

"Probably some bum trying to get a handout when the soup kitchen I support is just around the corner," Josh muttered under his breath and drove on, his mind now focused on making a grocery store run and buying sandwiches for Cindy's and his lunch.

It was ten a.m. when Josh pulled into his driveway, with Cindy not far behind. He hoped she noticed the BMW following them at a distance. He sighed with relief when she drove on past his driveway to make the drive around the corn field perimeter. The vehicle occupied by the driver and two companions kept going straight through the intersection instead of following her. They were both laughing when Cindy arrived to park her truck inside his garage. "Looks like we dodged the bullet again," said Josh.

"I feel like I'm on the secret military recon mission mentioned in a previous phone conversation," joked Cindy as Josh pushed the button to lower the garage door. "Just remember to watch out for buried land mines," he responded. "Obviously, I did not do any mine sweeping in the garage between now and last night." Cindy took a closer look around the area and found it necessary to agree. The garage was a mass of tables and floor stacked with tools, wood scraps and miscellaneous items used in the architect and construction trades, not to mention cobweb-filled windows badly in need of washing.

"Looks like we need to do more than rearrange living room furniture," Cindy commented.

Josh blushed sheepishly. "You would think, with me being an architect and management consultant for multimillion dollar projects, that I would be able to at least keep this mess under control. You wouldn't be interested in helping me organize this mess, would you? I would be willing to pay you."

"How about trade?" she suggested before hurrying to add, "I help you organize things out here, and you help me fill in a rut between my driveway and the county road."

Josh wasn't thinking this kind of trade. If he voiced his thoughts, there was little doubt they would have been a put off to Cindy if he said what he was thinking. "Sounds like I'm getting the better deal, but okay," he replied trying not to be embarrassed by his first thoughts.

"I'm glad you think so, but I would guess it will require getting permission from the highway department supervisor since my driveway abuts a county road." Cindy replied. "I'm sure he will require some sort of permit for a drainage tile, even though there has never been one at that location any time I can recall in all the years I've lived there."

"I take it back. I may not be getting the better deal, but since I agreed to help and am a man of my word, I will take proper steps to correct your rut," replied Josh.

"Even if that takes greasing the palms of certain county employees?" she questioned.

"Even then, but lady you are going to earn every penny it costs me. You have seen only the surface of what is involved in cleaning out and organizing this garage! Before you take a closer look and change your mind, step inside the house so we can then take care of rearranging the living room furniture."

"Not before getting cleaning supplies and vacuum cleaner from my truck bed," she replied. Oh dear, thought Josh. She must have seen dusty corners and dead flies filling windowsills when she was here last night. If she noticed them, she is bound to have seen dirty kitchen cupboards, window and floor and decided I do not own a vacuum cleaner or cleaning supplies.

Four hours later, including brief time taken to eat lunch, the living room, dining room and kitchen became spotless, and furniture was properly rearranged. When Cindy offered to clean three bedrooms and den yet today, Josh nixed the idea. "Those areas can wait for another day when I have time to clean. I didn't expect you to do double duty as a cleaning woman, also cleaning the dining room and kitchen, when you thought you were coming here to arrange living room furniture," said Josh. Cindy pushed back a strand of fallen hair from her eyes. "I am not one to rearrange furniture in a room in need of a good cleaning," she replied defiantly. "Bedrooms and den next week if you don't get around to cleaning them?" she questioned. "By the way, I checked. The bag in your vacuum cleaner needs emptying." The way she said it, eyes flashing and a winning smile, Josh did not take it as a rebuke to his poor housekeeping skills. He opted to disregard the memory his deceased wife Janice was the last person to have used it more than a year before cancer took her life. "I'll think about emptying the vacuum, but only if you will stay and have dinner with me," he replied.

"And what do you propose to prepare? All I saw was week-old bread, half a jar of peanut butter, canned soups, and coffee in the pantry. I won't even comment on what was in the refrigerator because it was unidentifiable," countered Cindy.

"I stopped at the grocery store and bought a couple jars of spaghetti sauce and some spaghetti before ordering the sandwiches, unless you don't mind heating up a frozen aged casserole," offered Josh as he slapped a hand to his forehead." Oh my gosh! I forgot to bring a sack in from the truck bed, including ice cream and vegetables needed for a tossed salad. Guess I was concentrating on the bag of sandwiches I put on the seat next to me. Any chance you like wilted salad and melted ice cream?" he asked with a boyish grin.

"Only if the lettuce is leaf style straight from my garden accompanied by shredded hard boiled eggs and hot bacon dressing. How about I take the sauce and pasta to my house and make a fresh salad to go with the spaghetti? I think there is still enough leaf lettuce left growing out in the garden to make a salad. Sorry, we ate all the chocolate cake for lunch, but there are snickerdoodles and frozen vanilla ice cream with hot fudge sauce for dessert." Josh didn't miss the emphasis on frozen in reference to ice cream.

"How can I refuse such an offer? Any chance we can have dinner outside on the lovely patio I saw when clearing your driveway and front yard after the storm? Evenings continue to be pleasant if we eat early, say about five before the sun goes down completely?"

"Only if you are willing to take the chance we will not be seen," replied Cindy. "You know my patio is not far from the road. That makes us easy targets for rubberneckers who happen to drive by to spy and draw conclusions."

"I say we go for it and give the gossips something to gossip about," replied Josh defiantly.

"I'm game if you are," replied Cindy. She wasn't game. What she wanted was to spend time with Josh getting to know him before she made the mistake of developing feelings for him beyond those already racing around inside her head. Josh offered to help her load the cleaning supplies into her truck, along with the vacuum cleaner. "Leave those things here," she replied. "I have a strong feeling I'm going to need them next week when we clean the garage, bedrooms and den." Josh backed off. Cindy could not help but see him smiling at her response.

"See you at five this evening?" he questioned to make sure she continued to be willing to cook.

Cindy grinned. "Not so fast! How about four-thirty so you can pick the last of the leaf lettuce from my garden?" she replied. "Hand me the sauce and spaghetti so I can take it with me and start cooking hamburger and onions to add to the sauce after I get home. Unless you have a compost pile hidden somewhere among the bushes out back, I'll take those wilted vegetables for my compost pile. Next week I'll be expecting a full pantry and well stocked refrigerator here at your house!"

I like the sound of that, even it means a grocery shopping trip thought Josh with a mock salute and heartfelt, "Yes ma'am."

Ten minutes past four Josh pulled in front of Cindy's garage. He arrived early with no intention of her opening the garage door allowing him to pull his truck inside beside her truck. The garage door began to open anyway. She stuck her head out the open door leading from the kitchen into the garage. "You are early," she called. "I didn't get the chance to fully open the garage door before you arrived. It will only take a minute to open completely then you can pull inside."

"I thought we were going to give the gossip mongers something to gossip about," he called back. "My truck stays out here."

Cindy grimaced. "Have it your way, but be ready for the consequences, plus the door needs to be open so you can come inside the kitchen to give you a basket for the lettuce. I'll fry the bacon needed for the dressing while you fill the basket about half full of lettuce. Garden is around back on the right side of the house." She met him at the doorway carrying a peck basket, the kind usually reserved for apples or peaches. He looked at the basket. "Isn't that basket large for just two people?" he questioned.

"The lettuce will wilt to half whatever you pick when the hot bacon dressing hits it," she explained. "You can rinse the lettuce with the hose attached to the house. I don't use pesticides, so that should take care of insects or dirt. Give the basket a vigorous shake to rid some of the water."

Twenty minutes later Josh returned to the kitchen with the basket less than half full of lettuce dripping water all over the tile floor. Cindy sighed and shook her head. "I should have told you to call me when you came back into the garage. I could have met you with tea towels to soak up the water remaining on the lettuce." Josh gave her a crestfallen look. "Forgive me. I'm a city boy who doesn't know the rules. I'm used to salads in packages from the grocery or in salad bowls ready to eat when served at restaurants.

Cindy smiled to change the mood. "Well, city boy, let's hope you know the business end of a mop! It's on the hanger beside the kitchen door in the garage." Josh didn't waste any time to mop up the mess he created.

"What about the basket? Isn't there something I can do to keep it from falling apart?" he asked.

"It will dry. Just leave it sitting in the garage. You can take plates, silverware, and glasses out to the patio table while I finish the salad," she instructed.

"You sure are bossy for such a pretty woman," replied Josh, reaching for the plates topped with two each of spoons, knives, forks and salad bowls. "What, no pasta bibs?" he joked. He ducked when she playfully tossed a dish towel at him.

"What do you think this is, some fancy trattoria in Italy? You are lucky I'm not using paper plates, plastic utensils and plastic glasses for iced tea," she replied with a look meant to be sour. The accompanying comical cross-eyed grin made the fake sour look fail so miserably it caused Josh to burst out laughing and playfully toss the dish towel back at her. "Touché!" she replied.

At a quarter past five, Cindy announced dinner was ready. Josh thought about teasing her for being later than the five o'clock dinner time agreed upon at his house. Wisely, he thought better of it, lest making such comments spoil the festive air. *No sense stirring up trouble where none exits*, he thought. "This salad is great!" he announced after helping himself twice. Wiping a dribble of dressing off his chin with the red and white checked cloth napkin Cindy thought to provide at the last minute, he praised her efforts. "You should bottle and sell this dressing," he commented.

No sooner were the words out his mouth when a carload of men driving a beat-up black Honda braked to a screeching stop in front of Cindy's house. They began to shout, hoot, and make rude hand gestures in their direction. "Would you look at that," yelled the driver. "Hey mister, how did you get lucky enough to have dinner with a hot babe like Cindy Marsh? We hear she only puts out on Monday, Wednesday, and Friday and this is Saturday!" Those seated in the car roared with drunken laughter. "Hey Cindy, how 'bout you reserve your patio table for me tomorrow night?" he slurred. "Better yet, why don't you reserve your bedroom? I'll bet I can keep going longer, harder, and faster than the old man sitting there on your patio tonight. How about giving me a try, Cindy babe?" taunted the driver.

Josh placed his napkin on the table, stood and started walking toward the car. The driver, once seeing his muscular build, stepped on the gas and sent loose gravel flying followed by a screech of rubber that left black tire marks on the pavement. Josh could hear sounds associated with drunken laughter coming from the car as it roared off into the distance. When he returned to the table, Cindy was holding the napkin to her face to hide her distress. Between sobs she reminded him this is what could happen. "I think it's time we take the remainder of our dinners inside before they return," she said.

"Come on, Cindy. We knew this could happen, and I'm sorry. If you want to go inside go, but I'm staying out here to finish this delicious meal," Josh responded. Cindy wiped her eyes with the napkin. A determined look replaced her tears. "Not on your life! I am NOT going inside! We said we were going to give people something to talk about, and that is exactly what we are going to do! Take a good look to the east. Isn't that Sharon's BMW coming down the road? She must have hired a pilot and plane to fly over my house to alert her when I have guests. I say we give her an eye full!"

"That's the spirit, Cindy! I say we give her the middle finger salute when she drives by," declared Josh with enthusiasm.

"I say we give her the finger along with the fist shake, Italian style. After all, we are having pasta," she answered with an equally defiant look mimicking the look on Josh's face. And that is exactly what they did while waving the red and white checkered napkins furiously with their free left hands. Shocked by their behavior, Sharon did not stick around. They knew she could hardly wait to add more rumors, but they didn't care.

"I have an even better idea," stated Josh as soon as Sharon drove away. "Just for kicks why don't you take me home. I'll leave my truck parked in front of your garage. Then we can both show up for church in the morning and sit in the same pew side by side."

Cindy laughed until tears ran down her cheeks. "I think it's a good idea, but don't you think it is going a little too far? How are you going to get to church if your truck is parked here?"

"It will be worth the three mile walk from my house to the church just to see Sharon's face," replied Josh with a wicked grin. Taking a chance, he added, "Or I could spend the night in the guest room again."

Cindy took a deep breath. "I don't think it's a wise decision," she replied. She wanted to say, "Yes you can stay, but not in the guest room." Instead, she answered, "I think it would be best for both our sakes if you went home. I also think it's time for snickerdoodles, ice cream and hot fudge sauce."

"How about adding coffee and TV to go with dessert?" asked Josh. "That would keep me and my truck here long enough to make a point if Sharon or that carload of idiots have the guts to come back to take another look." Cindy just nodded and with trembling hands gathered up their now empty plates and tableware to make a quick exit across the patio toward the house.

She was standing in front of the kitchen sink staring out the window when Josh followed carrying salad bowls and glasses with a napkin tossed over his arm giving the appearance of a waiter. "I am zee waiter here to do your bidding, Madam," he said in a bad Italian accent. "Anything Madam wishes of me I will do." Lost in silent meditation, the sound of his voice caused Cindy to utter a scream and jump involuntarily. Josh quickly found a place to deposit items he was carrying on the kitchen table and take her in his arms. "I'm sorry. I didn't mean to scare you," he said without offering to let her go, instead holding her closer to his chest. Even though she was not expecting his reaction, Cindy did not move to free his embrace right away. Instead, she stood staring into his bedazzling green eyes for just a moment before stepping away. "I . . . I think it's time for cookies and ice cream, then time for you to leave," she said softly while disengaging his arms to step away.

"I think it's time for me to leave now," replied Josh huskily when it was the last thing he wanted to do. He groaned softly when Cindy leaned forward and kissed him on the cheek. "You are right. I think it's time for you to leave and for me to clean up this kitchen," she replied in an equally husky voice before taking another step back from him, thinking, *I don't know what got into me! I should not have kissed him.*

Josh's truck was still parked in front of Cindy's garage when the sun rose the next morning. He fried bacon and scrambled eggs as Cindy set the breakfast table, made toast and brewed coffee. And yes, they sat side by side at church, trying to control their laughter at the sight of Sharon's disapproving glare when walking past them to her usual seat. They both knew Sharon drove by Cindy's house that morning to see Josh's parked truck where he left it last night. It gave

Cindy a sense of satisfaction that the busybody didn't know Josh spent the night in one of the guest rooms.

CHAPTER NINE

Monday morning dawned clear and sunny. Along with it came an unusual heat wave for late September. Along with the heat came a flock of buzzards circling over the hospital construction site in response to the foul odor associated with decay. "What the hell!" exclaimed Melvin Prendergast after parking his SUV in the area that would become the paved parking lot adjacent to the new hospital wing. It was not necessary for him to ask where the stench was originating. Melvin knew. What he did not know was why the concrete scheduled to be poured in the footers early the previous Saturday morning had not taken place.

"Hey, you!" he called, directing those words toward one of the workers standing apart from the others. "Why in the hell weren't the footers poured on Saturday morning, and where is Josh Morgan? I need to have a word with him right now!" demanded Melvin.

The man shrugged his shoulders. He was used to dealing with men wearing suits, white shirts and ties, along with their demanding ways. "How should I know? I'm not the one who ordered the concrete. I was hired to do cleanup," he responded. "Josh called the site foreman to say he would be late. You need to talk to the foreman."

"Where is the foreman and what is his name?" demanded Melvin, pretending he didn't notice the nauseating smell and circling birds of prey coupled with his sudden urge to vomit.

"He's the one over there in the green shirt studying blueprints trying to find out where that awful smell in coming from. "His name is Abe," replied the construction worker. He pointed to a group of men talking and looking at what appeared to be blueprints. Melvin did not bother to thank him for the information before heading toward the small group clustered around a tall, lean, muscular man holding a set of blueprints. It took a moment for Melvin to note two other men were also wearing green work shirts. "Which one of you is Abe?" he demanded.

"That depends on who wants to know," replied the man holding the blueprints. Melvin puffed out his chest in a feeble effort to make him appear formidable, a look reminding Abe of a plump Banty rooster strutting his stuff for the hens.

"That would be me. My name is Melvin Pendergast. Mr. Pendergast to you! I am the hospital Chairman of the Board. Am I to assume you are Abe?" Abe merely nodded. "And pray tell me, why are you and these men standing around doing nothing! Are you waiting for Josh Morgan to show up and lead all of you around by the hand?"

The workmen started to walk away. Abe stopped them. He bristled and crossed his well-defined muscled arms across his chest, the rolled-up blueprints securely tucked under them. "Since when does someone who has no idea what it takes to construct a multi-story concrete and steel building tell me and my crew what they should be doing? In case you are interested, we were taking a serious look at what else they could be doing, since the concrete pour has been rescheduled for Friday due to a shortage of materials, and we are trying to locate possible locations where the terrible smell is coming from and fix it," said Abe in a less than friendly manner.

"How dare you speak to me in that tone! I happen to own a real estate company in addition to serving the community on the hospital board of directors! I'll have you fired before you know what is happening!" declared Melvin indignantly. He failed to see or hear footsteps walking up behind him.

"What is going on here?" asked Josh.

"This insolent barbarian just informed me I have no right to question five men standing around doing nothing while awaiting your late arrival," snarled Melvin.

Josh stifled a sigh. "First of all, Mr. Prendergast, Abe is not a barbarian. He is the very able foreman on this job, and we are lucky to have him. If members of his crew are gathered around him checking blueprints, there is a good reason. And from the terrible smell, I assume they are trying to locate where the smell is originating. There could have been a break in an existing sewer line during the use of a backhoe leveling the parking area in preparation for paving."

Melvin continued to glare at him. "I suppose you hired someone cheap to do the leveling work so you could brag to other hospital board members how you are saving money," Melvin stated hotly.

Josh felt mounting anger. "You know I would never do such a thing! If a sewer line was hit, it is the fault of the town council's approved inspector, a council on which you serve, who improperly marked existing sewer lines to prevent such things from happening!"

Realizing he could not refute this response, Melvin changed the subject. "What in tarnation happened to the concrete footer pour supposed to have happened early Saturday morning?" he demanded, trying to disregard increasing numbers of buzzards circling above the site or sweat accumulating on his upper lip. Josh repeated the information he had been given. Hearing this news, Melvin began to really sweat. He counted on the concrete pour happening on Saturday morning to hide Jude's body. That was not going to happen before decaying remains were bound to be found. He did not have the faintest idea what to do next. In a state of panic, he turned and walked away without saying another word, jumped in his car then backed out of the lot to drive away at a high rate of speed.

Josh turned to Abe. "I'm sorry about him being so rude and nasty. Speaking of nasty, where is that terrible smell coming from?"

"We haven't tracked it down yet, but we will soon," replied Abe. "In the meantime, what do you want me and the rest of the crew to do since we can't start the steel framework until after the concrete cures with steel anchor plates in place. It doesn't look like the pour is going to happen until the end of the week at the earliest."

Josh scratched the side of his face in thought. "After you find the source of the smell and take care of it, you and the rest of the crew take paid vacation until those footers cure. I know all of you put in extra hours without asking for overtime. There is enough left in the budget to compensate all of you for a few days off. I hate to ask, but could you and the other men take turns acting as night watchman? I noticed cement blocks we piled over there for the front steps foundation underpinnings are missing." Abe looked in the direction where Josh pointed and shook his head in disgust. "Sure thing, boss. I'll take first shift tonight and assign each of the other men to a shift based on seniority."

"Tell those working they will be paid their regular hourly rate in addition to vacation pay," said Josh.

"Did anyone ever tell you that you are one hell of a boss?" replied Abe.

Josh laughed. "I've been told to go to hell, but as for telling me I'm one hell of a boss, that hasn't happened until now. Thanks man. I appreciate it."

"What are you going to do on your time off?" asked Abe.

Josh felt himself blush. "I was thinking about going fishing over at Mirror Lake Thursday afternoon." He did not add this would only happen if a certain lady agreed to accompany him.

"I love to fish. Would you like some company on Thursday?" asked Abe. When Josh hesitated, Abe smiled. "I think you might have plans for another fishing companion, if what I've been hearing is true."

"And what have you been hearing?" asked Josh.

"Nothing much . . . just that you and Cindy Marsh are shacking up. And that's okay with me," he quickly added. "It's about time you started thinking about finding someone, and Cindy is one fine looking lady, and she is nice, too. Personally, I think it's past the time she should be finding herself a good man in her life like you."

"Where did you hear Cindy and I were shacking up?" asked Josh, as if he didn't already know. Abe gave a knowing look. "You must be kidding! I've only been on the job here for a little over a year, but I've learned everybody knows that woman Sharon Murphy keeps tabs on everyone. If it isn't her, it's a woman named Betty. Sorry, I don't remember her last name."

"Prendergast," muttered Josh in disgust.

"Isn't that the same last name as the asshole who just called me a barbarian and tried to tell me how to do my job?" questioned Abe.

"You got it," replied Josh. "Two of Riverwood's finest when it comes to spreading rumors. I could name a few more if you would like." Before Abe could reply, Josh walked across the unpaved parking area, climbed in his truck, and drove away thinking, *I should not have slept in the guest room on Saturday night when Cindy and I had dinner on her patio. I have the feeling I could have shared her bed if I pushed the idea. But taking such action would put our friendship in jeopardy. I don't think Cindy is the type to go for a one-night stand, so put those thoughts out of your mind, or you could lose her trust in less than a heartbeat.*

CHAPTER TEN

Melvin Prendergast found himself driving aimlessly around back country roads trying to calm his nerves after leaving the construction site. "This isn't getting me anywhere," he said, continuing to talk aloud to himself. "I need to go back to the real state office and talk to Gracie. She can help me figure out a way to handle Jude's death. I need to make sure we get our stories straight. There isn't any doubt his body will be found, probably today." With those thoughts going through his mind, he turned the car around on the narrow road, almost ending up in the deep ditch meant to drain the soybean field when heavy rains or snowmelt hit, adding a few choice words during the process. A few more choice words spewed from his mouth after arriving at his office to find no sign of Grace. She had not come to work, nor did she bother to call Melvin to say she was not coming. Grace was busy getting ready to list her house for sale in preparation for moving into the promised condo on Mirror Lake if she kept her mouth shut. She went so far as to place a handmade for sale sign in her front yard rather than split the brokerage fee using a business sign from the office. "I'm not about to split the fee with Melvin," she muttered. Expecting his call about an hour after usual opening time at the office, she allowed the phone to ring longer than necessary just to fluster her boss. "Hello," was all she said instead of identifying herself.

"Gracie, its Melvin. Where in the hell are you? Why aren't you at the office? She hated it when he referred to her as Gracie.

"My name is Grace, not Gracie," she informed him coldly. "What do you want?"

"I want you to come to work is what I want," he replied, trying not to sound harried.

"I'll be in later, but not until after I finish some business here," she replied.

"And what business is more important than the business here at the real estate office?" he inquired.

"Oh, I think you know. There are certain things required when you are selling your home and moving; things you should be aware of since you own a real estate company; a real estate company with condos on the lake front, like the condo you promised me, along with a partnership in the company." Grace's comments were met by dead silence. "What's the matter, Melvin? Cat got your tongue, or did you already forget what you promised to keep me quiet? If you forgot, I am willing, ready, and able to remind you and anyone else who presses me for answers regarding who shot Jude and who dumped his body in the footer!" Grace kept talking without allowing Melvin a chance to respond. "I expect you to have a bill of sale ready for both our signatures with me listed as paid in full owner of a first floor, lake front condo when I get back to the office. Then get busy writing the contract listing me half owner in the real estate business. Is that clear?" She, again, didn't wait for a reply before continuing, "And I expect you to visit at least twice a week once I move in. It won't be for tea and crumpets if you get my drift. Our little tryst on your office sofa reminded me of what I have been missing over the past twelve years since my husband's death."

Melvin felt as though he had been punched in the gut. "Grace, you can't be serious about me visiting you twice every week! How will I explain my absences to Betty? You know she keeps me on a short leash these days." Melvin didn't even try to hide fear in his voice.

Grace smiled to herself. "You are a very resourceful man. You will think of something to tell that nosy wife of yours. Now if you will excuse me, I need to finish the packing I've started." The phone line went dead.

Melvin put his head down on arms stretched across his solid mahogany desk and cried. "What have I gotten myself into?" he lamented. "That bitch not only wants a free condo and cut of the real estate business, but she also expects me to have sex with her twice a week? I'm lucky if I can get it up twice a month using Viagra most of the time!" When he raised his head and mopped his face with the sleeve of his shirt, a brownish red stain on the carpet next to his desk caught his eye. "What the hell? I thought Grace cleaned up the blood." Then he recalled she had cleaned it up, but blood must have soaked into the padding to resurface on the carpet; a reminder of what he had done. He took a deep breath, got up and went to the janitorial closet to get supplies necessary to clean the large area again. "I should not be doing this," he grumbled. "Cleaning is woman's work." At the same time, he knew better than to ask Grace to clean the area again.

Two weeks later, Grace, having sold her house in town and pocketed the proceeds, including the full listing fee, moved into her new fully furnished lake front condo. She invited all the ladies from church to a housewarming party, including Melvin's wife Betty. She gave serious thought about not inviting Betty, then decided it would be fun to sit beside her knowing the woman did not have a clue about the deal, which included Grace having sex with her husband twice a week. *Serve's Betty right when she has spent the past twelve years spying on me by peeping through her curtains, calling me at night whenever she fails to see a light on, or my car drive out of the garage when she thinks I should be home. I wonder how Melvin is going to pull off those visits without being caught dipping his wick in my cookie jar?* Those thoughts started her laughing uncontrollably, which caused Ellie Montgomery, sitting on the other side of her on the sofa, to ask what was so funny. "Oh, I was just thinking about a cookie jar. You know one of those that looks like a pig," she replied. Ellie, along with Betty seated nearby, wondered if Grace was on drugs.

"I think I'll have another piece of that delicious chocolate cake Cindy brought," Ellie replied as she got up from the sofa. She added, "I'm surprised Cindy decided to attend your housewarming. She hardly ever attends any functions since Harold died." She took a breath before deciding to add, "Did you per chance notice these past several weeks she regularly attends church and sits next to Josh Morgan in the back row pew?"

Grace forced the expected frown in response. "I noticed. Isn't it shameful the way those two are always leaving church together before the pastor finishes the benediction? I often wonder where they go. Sharon Murphy told me she sees Josh's truck parked in front of Cindy's garage on an almost nightly basis, and it is still there early the next morning. You don't suppose they are having an affair, do you?" Ellie arched her right eyebrow ever so slightly. Seeing the arched eyebrow, Grace thought Ellie knew for sure Cindy and Josh were having an affair. This thought made her giggle again, making Ellie and Betty uncomfortable enough to seek conversation with other guests.

Grace continued to sit observing everyone following Ellie and Betty's departure. It gave her pleasure to think sex is not just for the young. It's for a smart old broad like me when she's been a witness to murder, but that's for me to know and not for the likes of you two to find out. Sometimes even a homely old broad like me can get lucky, if you consider having sex with the likes of Melvin Prendergast being lucky. With that thought in mind, Grace stood, a giddy smile on her face, to leave Ellie and Betty standing across the room staring in her direction and even more certain Grace was on some sort of medication. They had no idea when Grace walked past them in order to mingle with other guests that she was gloating at what she perceived was their jealousy at her sudden change of fortune. She could not help thinking, *I wonder how these good Christian ladies will react when they see my name appear on the real estate office building door? Good luck explaining that one Melvin, especially to your wife!*

CHAPTER ELEVEN

Chill filled the air on the mid-October day. A month had passed. Yellow crime scene tapes marking the place where Jude Prichard's body had been found under eight cement blocks at the bottom of a footer were now removed. Clothing his wife described he had been wearing the day he left for work, in addition to dental records, confirmed his identity to the satisfaction of the coroner and sheriff. Damage to the body by the cement blocks and decomposition made visual identification impossible. The closed casket funeral was attended by almost everyone comprising the church congregation. This was out of respect for his widow and children, not necessarily out of respect for Jude. The footer had since been filled with cement, steel beams reaching skyward. Reporters and the curious no longer congregated three-deep around the site. The coroner did issue a statement to the fact Jude had been shot in the heart at close range. No gun was found, making the determination of murder. A suspect had not yet been identified. It was not for lack of trying on the part of Sheriff Simon Heinz. He systematically interrogated at least half the town's population over the past month. His main concentration focused on Josh Morgan; a position taken when he failed to take information seriously when a drifter came forward to identify a possible suspect in both murders, something the sheriff would later regret.

For the sixth time in less than a month, the sheriff arrived at the construction site demanding to speak with Josh. "Tell me again where you were around the time Jude went missing," asked the barrel chested, pot-bellied stockily built man known for an intimidating attitude. "Like I told you the five times you have already interrogated me Sheriff, I was here doing my job at the work site, at home watching TV, or having a meal at the diner with a friend. Why is it so difficult for you to understand my answers?" stated Josh, trying to keep his frustration at bay.

"I might be inclined to quit asking if you were to name your friend with whom you have those meals," replied the unsmiling sheriff.

"My private life is none of your business," Josh answered in a barely civil tone. "Why do you keep beating around the bush? We both know the reason you are harassing me has nothing to do with Jude's death. The construction crew verified my whereabouts, along with two waitresses at the diner where I bought a sack meal around the time the coroner believes Jude died. I returned to the work site to eat with several other workers. Be honest. You want revenge. You still think I had something to do with my wife's death, even though the coroner stated unequivocally he found no evidence to that fact."

The sheriff averted looking directly at Josh when he answered, "That is a supposition on your part."

"Can you look me squarely in the eyes and tell me it isn't any more of a supposition than you trying to pin Jude's death on me because I wasn't born in this town, along with rumors I overdosed Janice with morphine? How many locals have you interrogated more times than me?" questioned Josh. The sheriff could not come up with a ready answer, so he turned to leave, but not before saying, "I will get to the bottom of this death, even if I have to interrogate you a hundred times, and you can quote me on that!"

"Interrogate me all you want. Just be aware I will take legal action against you for harassment. I realize you believe you are the protector of the peace in this county and the town of Rockwood. You need to remember this is a small area in the scheme of things. In this state there are other avenues in which to file charges against you. You are a big fish in a small pond, so unless you have proof to take before the grand jury, leave me alone and let me do the job I was hired to do!" There was no doubt Josh was angry while trying to remain relatively civil as he turned and walked away. Raising the sheriff's ire and awareness Josh could seek a remedy to stop harassment must have worked. The sheriff did not contact him again regarding Jude's demise.

Instead, he turned his focus on Cindy Marsh playing the role of good cop. This tactic changed when he didn't get expected responses to his questions, prompting him to become more aggressive in his approach. "Ms. Marsh, we all know you and Josh Morgan are engaged in an affair. Doesn't this mean you would say or do anything to protect him, including lie about his whereabouts on the day of Jude's death?" he asked, standing with one foot on the bottom porch step of Cindy's house. Cindy made it a point to make him feel he did not have a choice except to stand there when she didn't invite him to come onto the porch or come inside. She quickly figured out he did not have cause for obtaining a warrant. If he had one, he would have waved it in her face, insisting he come inside to question her.

"How dare you accuse me of having an affair with Josh Morgan or accuse me of lying about his whereabouts! At the time the coroner determined Jude died, we didn't even have dinner together that night. He worked late. I ate dinner alone here at the house. Josh and I are just friends who happen to enjoy the company of one another. We've also had meals here at my house. So what? Is it illegal to have a meal with a friend without town gossips deciding we are having an affair? I don't think the word affair applies when two unmarried people decide to enjoy one another's company or attend church together."

The sheriff raised his thick busy eyebrows. "Just friends? I hardly think you two are just friends when his truck is often seen parked outside your garage late at night and is still there in the morning."

"I didn't realize it is against the law for me to have a friend stay overnight. Josh did spend one night in a guest room when it was impossible to move my truck until the driveway was cleared of fallen tree limbs back when we had that bad storm." She did not mention Josh had spent the night in the same room a second time. She felt it was none of the sheriff's business after there were no charges filed against him following his wife's death; therefore, no bearing on either murder investigation. "For the record, you can check the local towing service to confirm Josh's truck broke down at the church yard sale. He had it towed to Luke's Garage. I offered to take him home. What is so hard to understand about that? He fell into a deep sleep while seated in my truck. By the time we would have arrived at his house, I realized I could not awaken him without pulling off to the side of the road. This is when I decided to turn around and drive here to my house before the warned storm hit. Of course, this is when Sharon Murphy and her nosy friends just happened to drive by late the next morning trailing closely behind the county crew clearing the road. She must have seen Josh out in my lawn cutting fallen tree limbs in my driveway. Without knowing the facts, she and her cohorts decided we had spent the night together."

The sheriff cleared his throat. "Well, when two unmarried people of the opposite sex are observed cohabitating in the same house overnight, that usually means there is more than just friendship, unless they are family members. Why, Sharon Murphy and her friends have been seeing Josh's truck parked in front of your garage late at night and early the next morning more times than any of them can recall. Does this mean you are willing to provide an alibi for Josh?" His response infuriated her.

"Didn't I just tell you Josh spent the night in my guest room the night of the storm?" she questioned, emphasizing the word guest. "Sheriff, unless you are here to charge me with being an accomplice to murder, I think you need to get the hell off my property and don't come back without a warrant or a damn good reason to take me to jail! It would appear you are no better than Sharon Murphy or her minions when it comes to spreading rumors! Unless Sharon broke into my house, which is illegal, and observed Josh and I sharing the same bed engaging in compromising behavior, how does she know what happens in my house, let alone in my bedroom? Just in case you are interested, Josh has been helping me with plans to build a new shop in the rundown section of town. We are in the planning stage of giving tourists a reason to come here, besides that mud hole referred to as Mirror Lake! He is, after all, an architect and building consultant, not that you would be interested in being reminded of the fact he is also a law abiding, upstanding citizen who was hired to design and oversee the building of the new hospital wing! Sometimes he is here at my house well past midnight, then he goes home and returns before he goes to the hospital job site the next morning! Seeing his truck parked in front of my garage during those times is nobody's business but his and mine!" Cindy regretted referring to Mirror Lake as a mud hole. The lake is a lovely 175-acre, 100-foot deep, spring fed body of water regularly stocked with edible fish. She called it a mud hole to irritate the sheriff. Knowing he was proud of the fact he organized routine cleanup activities to keep it and the shoreline pristine, she was not about to apologize for making such a statement.

"Now Ms. Marsh, don't get all upset. I am talking to everyone, not just you, in a serious effort to solve a murder. It just seems strange Jude Prichart's body was concealed at the site where Josh spends a lot of time. It is a known fact Melvin wanted Josh fired and replaced by Jude. That could be a reason for Josh to get rid of the competition," insisted the sheriff. Cindy looked at him like he had just fallen off a turnip truck. "Competition? Jude Prichart? You must be out of your friggin' mind! Jude couldn't begin to hold a candle to Josh when it comes to construction! You don't seem to be having any trouble believing rumors provided by the likes of Sharon Murphy, so why don't you focus on rumors Jude didn't know his ass from a hole in the ground when it came to construction? Since you seem to be dealing in rumors, I'm sure you must have heard other hospital board members laughed Melvin out of the room without a second to his motion to fire Josh!"

The sheriff's face turned bright red. "Ms. Marsh! There's no need for swearing!" He had nothing to say about lack of support by hospital board members when Melvin made a motion to fire Josh and hire Jude. Cindy wasn't about to take his response.

"Just like there is no need for you to go around spreading rumors Josh might have killed Jude, or that Josh and I are having an affair when you don't have proof of either one! And don't you dare tell me what words I can use! If I need to make a point concerning what I've said and it takes swear words, that's what I will use! If men can use them, why can't I? Have you forgotten this not 1930 when women were expected to remain silent, barefoot and pregnant while standing in front of the kitchen stove cooking meals, or down on their knees scrubbing clothes on a washboard for the man of the house?" By this time Cindy was shaking. This was not due to fear. Her response was based on the fact she was so angry.

Sheriff Heinz, taken aback by her outburst, removed his foot off the step and stepped away, fearful she might take a swing at him. "Ms. Marsh, Cindy, I can see that you are upset and I'm sorry, but it's my job to . . ."

Cindy cut him off. "It's your job to protect the citizens of this county and the town of Riverwood. You have interrogated me. I have given you truthful answers, so why don't you move along and do the job for which taxpayers like me pay your salary? And by the way, tell your deputy Pete Clossin to stop peeping in my windows and asking if he can come inside for a drink, and as he put it, 'have some bedroom fun!'"

Taken off guard by her accusation regarding one of his deputies, Sheriff Heinz tried to think of a way he could legally arrest Cindy. He came up empty knowing there wasn't a law against anyone speaking their mind, even if they used a swear word or two. Besides, she was a born area resident with a reputation for helping people in need in addition to what he believed were lies told by Sharon Murphy. Everyone who knew Cindy liked her, the only exception being Sharon Murphy, a vindictive, dried up old biddy who didn't have a life, and several others who kowtowed to her out of fear she would turn her wrath onto them if they didn't follow her lead. Cindy had not threatened bodily harm or touched him, so he knew his hands were tied.

"You can be sure I will speak to Pete," replied the sheriff.

I'm sure you will, Cindy thought in disgust. When she turned her back toward him to reinforce her forceful verbal demand to leave her property immediately, he took the not-so-subtle hint and left.

After the sheriff drove away, Cindy sat down on the top porch step and put her head in her hands. "Take some deep breaths," she told herself. "You don't have to relive what happened over the past few years, including today." As much as she wanted to forget, she knew it was impossible. Today was one of those days when unwanted memories came flooding back. The sheriff's questioning and allegations, coupled with thoughts of what might have been had Harrold lived, made it seem like events happening over a lifetime were still very much in motion. Saddest of all, there was not much she could do to make them stop.

Harold Marsh was diagnosed with an aggressive form of untreatable leukemia three years after he and Cindy were married. He died in his sleep two months following diagnosis. Cindy found herself alone, unwilling to continue living the carefree lifestyle she and Harold once lived since he became part of her life. She stopped attending parties, fishing at the lake or meeting girlfriends for lunch. She attended church on a sporadic basis. Having lost faith, she quite often left during a sermon and always before the end of the benediction. She stopped using makeup or having her hair styled at the salon, instead tying it up in a ponytail with a rubber band to keep it out of her face. In the past year she went on two dates with men who turned out to have only one thing on their mind, getting into her bed. She made it clear this was not going to happen before sending them on their way.

"Then I made the mistake of going to the church yard sale where I met Josh Morgan," she lamented aloud. "Why couldn't I have learned to live with those items we spent more than three years accumulating? Why was I so dead set on trying to wipe out memories we made together? Why was I attracted to Josh Morgan? I knew I would be asking for rumor mongers like Sharon Murphy and her crowd to have a field day at my expense." Cindy continued to sit on the porch step asking herself these questions well past time for dinner. Only when she began to feel a chill as the last colors of the sunset faded did she go inside to make a cup of instant coffee. After drinking the coffee, she thought about preparing something to eat, opened the refrigerator door, took a quick look inside and closed it. Nothing in there appealed to her. Thinking she would go downstairs into the den and watch television to settle her nerves, she grabbed a bag of potato chips from the pantry, then returned to the refrigerator for a bottle of soda before opening the door to make the trip downstairs into the den. There she settled among a pile of pillows on the beige leather sofa, covered her legs with a turquoise throw, then turned on the TV. Upset and distracted, she did not make her usual check to make sure the front door was locked.

The clock on the den wall registered ten minutes past ten p.m. when she sat up, startled at the sound of footsteps coming down the stairs into the den. In a state of fear, she grabbed the soda bottle to use as a weapon. She swore softly, remembering the shotgun was in the kitchen, the pistol in the lamp table drawer in her bedroom. "Who's there?" she called.

"It's me, Josh. When I didn't see any lights on, I tried the front door. It was unlocked, so I came inside thinking something might have happened to you when I called out and didn't get an answer. That sent me on a search of the house to end up down here. Did you forget we were meeting this evening to go over plans for your new store?" Seeing the soda bottle in her hand he added, "I'm sorry if I frightened you, but would you please put that soda bottle down?"

Cindy was unaware she was still gripping the bottle with the intent of using it as a weapon. She leaned forward to deposit it on the coffee table. "I didn't forget about our meeting. I was exhausted and angry after my encounter with Sheriff Heinz earlier this evening. I came down here to watch TV and relax. I must have drifted off to sleep." Reluctant to say anything more about her encounter with the sheriff and risk upsetting Josh, she didn't say anything else.

Josh was not about to give up on an explanation. "And what did the sheriff have to say?" he asked, as if he did not already suspect. "Oh, you know, the usual when investigating a murder," she responded evasively.

"How well I know. He already interrogated me five, make it six times over the past month. I'm sure the two of you didn't chat about old times over a cup of tea."

Cindy smiled and wrinkled her nose. "As a matter of fact, I kept him standing, one foot on the bottom step of the front porch. I also spoke my mind using a couple of four-letter words he didn't like."

Josh gave an expression of approval. "You don't strike me as a person to use that kind of language, so he must have deserved it. Do you want to tell me what made you so angry?"

"Not really, but if you insist, sit and I'll tell you." Josh sat down close beside her on the sofa, his hands resting in his lap, to listen intently without saying a word until she finished speaking. Only then did he put his arm around her shoulder and pull her onto his lap. "I am sorry you are being subjected to all this simply because of contact with me." Cindy didn't make a move to slide off his lap as she would have done in the past. Instead, she kissed his cheek while glancing at the wall clock. "It's late. Would you like to spend the night in the guest room?" He did not hesitate to take her up on the offer after experiencing a trying day, and the way she was responding to his effort to comfort her. Try as he might, he couldn't help thinking he might get lucky. That thought evaporated when she slid off his lap to announce she was hungry, and would he like to join her in the kitchen for a grilled cheese sandwich. He took a deep breath before letting her know it was a good idea.

The next morning Josh was in the kitchen frying bacon, scrambling eggs and making toast while Cindy made coffee and set the breakfast nook table. Once again, Josh spent the night in one of the guest rooms, not exactly what he had hoped for, but at least he was in the same house with her. "Slow and steady wins the race, and she is worth waiting for," he recalled mumbling after slipping out of his clothes down to his underwear last night. Pulling back the covers, he knew he would spend a restless night alone with his thoughts. He was not alone spending a restless night.

Cindy, who usually slept at least several hours as soon as her head hit the pillow, watched the clock on the bedside table move its hands slowly from one hour to the next. She was not able to convince herself all she had to do was get the nerve to walk out of her bedroom, across the living room and down the hallway to join Josh in the guest room bed. At the same time, she knew now was not the right time for such an action. "He might think I'm a lonely woman lacking morals, serving to reinforce Sharon's unfounded rumors. As much as I would like to lie in his arms the remainder of the night, that is not the way to encourage an enduring relationship," she whispered into her pillow.

CHAPTER TWELVE

Melvin Prendergast was nervous, although he believed he was snowing the sheriff with glib answers during the interview concerning where he was at the time of Jude Prichart's death. "Why Sheriff, my secretary and I were working late on a big deal the night Jude was murdered. You can check it out with Grace. As a woman of character, she can vouch for both of us," he declared.

"Is that so? How did you conclude Jude was killed on the night you were working late when the coroner did not verify the exact time of death as day or night?" questioned the sheriff.

Melvin felt his pulse increase. "I assumed Jude was killed at night or the killer or killers would have been seen or heard the gunshot if it happened during daytime business hours, and wouldn't construction workers have noticed if someone tossed a body in the footer when on the job during the daytime? As far as I know none of them work after dark."

Sheriff Heinz nodded but let Melvin know he would be talking to Grace. This statement gave cause for Melvin to worry. He could not help wondering if Grace would crack under pressure. Even though he helped her move into the promised lakeside condo, he had not filed the deed, nor were papers drawn up naming her a partner in the real estate company. He knew this could pose a problem, but he wasn't ready to make good on those promises unless there was no alternative. Melvin breathed a sigh of relief when the sheriff declined the offer of a drink and left his office.

"Looks like I need to have a little talk with Gracie," mumbled Melvin with a shudder. "She is expecting me to . . . to show up and have sex with her tomorrow night, and its Betty's and my 26th wedding anniversary," he muttered aloud in frustration at the thought of having to have sex with Grace again. "Dear God in heaven! How am I going to satisfy two women on the same night?" Melvin continued to mumble as he fumbled with opening the lock on the door to his inner office liquor cabinet. He poured himself a double shot of expensive aged whiskey kept well hidden behind less expensive brands used to toast clients after a sale. Without blinking an eye, he downed it in one gulp. A few minutes later when that had not done the trick of diminishing his anxiety, he poured another double shot and downed it. Half an hour later he managed to lock the cabinet, walk unsteadily to the office entrance door and stumble down the office building steps while holding onto the metal railing. He was able to continue across the sidewalk to the curb, almost losing his balance while getting in his SUV to make the drive to the lakeside condo. "I'll have sex with Grace first since she is easy to please. That way I can be home in time for dinner with Betty by eight p.m. like I promised her," he mumbled. Red lights flashing from behind caught his attention. "Oh shit! This is all I need!" he slurred while fumbling in his inside jacket pocket for his wallet. With difficulty, he extracted the one-hundred-dollar bill he kept ready to hand to the deputy, along with his driver's license as he had done on previous occasions. Three minutes later he was on his way with a verbal warning not to drink and drive, having convinced the deputy he was on his way home just down the block. "Works every time," he slurred with an arrogant laugh as he continued driving to the lake. Two double shots of whiskey played a major factor in him forgetting to take the little blue pill while still in the office.

Unwilling to take any chance of being seen in the condo guest parking lot, Melvin parked in an empty carport attached to an unoccupied unit. He felt a sense of relief when he saw no lights on or cars parked next to the two condo units he knew were occupied at the far end of the complex. The only light showing at this end of the building was what passed for security lighting at the entrance in addition to minimal light filtering through simi-sheer curtains in Grace's ground floor living room. As soon as she answered his knock Melvin knew he was in trouble. Grace was not smiling, and he didn't have even a hint of an erection, having forgotten to take the little blue pill. Oh boy! I'm in deep trouble he thought. The look on Grace's face let him know she was not happy to see him when she answered the door.

"Why are you here early?" demanded Grace who was wearing only a bathrobe following a shower. "I thought we agreed for you to be here at six -thirty. It's only six! You can see I'm not ready for company, otherwise the porch light would have been on like we discussed."

"I . . . just couldn't wait to see you," he lied. This brought a smile to Grace's face, but it did not last. "That's nice, but I don't see an envelope in your hand containing my deed to this property or paperwork naming me partner in the real estate business. What gives?" she demanded.

"I must have left them at the office on my desk. You can pick them up when you come to work tomorrow." Grace edged around Melvin to slam the front door shut before turning to face him. Her actions left him to turn facing her in the foyer. "Tomorrow!" she shrieked. "Tomorrow is Saturday. You know I do not work Saturdays or Sundays anymore! What are you trying to pull?"

"I'm not trying to pull anything," insisted Melvin. "I was in a hurry thinking about, you know, having sex with you." He pulled her close in what turned out to be an effort in futility to verify that statement by grinding his pelvis against her pelvis. His "Johnson" was not responding, and Grace knew it.

"Let go of me you good for nothing bastard!" she shrieked, trying to wriggle loose. "I've seen more action in a carton of night crawlers at the bait store than what I'm feeling in your crotch! You don't have any intention of following through with our deal about me keeping quiet in Jude's death or having sex! Just where am I supposed to get the money to pay for this fancy condo? My house was only worth half what this place costs!" That said, she started pounding on Melvin's chest and continued to scream bloody murder using every foul word she could remember.

Suddenly Melvin felt his hands slip from around her waist and inch upward around her neck. He kept them there squeezing tighter and tighter until she became limp and stopped screaming before releasing his hold. In his inebriated state, he had no idea how long it had taken before Grace stopped struggling and slid out of his grip to slide to the floor in a heap. He bent down and tried shaking her with no response. He checked her neck for carotid artery pulse. There was none. He saw only red marks left by his hands on her skin and her milky blue eyes fixed in a vacant stare. Melvin staggered upright in terror when her tongue lolled out the side of her mouth. Once again, Melvin found himself saying, "Oh my God! What have I done?" Only this time Grace was in no condition to help him. It was up to him to dispose of her body, and he had less than an hour to do it before joining his wife to celebrate their anniversary.

Following dinner Later that evening, Betty was amazed at his sexual performance. "Why Melvin, darling, you are even more sexy than you were on our wedding night twenty-six years ago," she declared. "I don't want to know if you took one of those little blue pills. If so, keep taking it." She didn't know Melvin had taken two pills, returning to his office to take them before driving home. Melvin rolled off her with a groan amid thoughts including, *I am not sure you want me to take your advice seriously.*

Three days later, Grace's body, clad in only an open bathrobe, was found floating face down in Mirror Lake. Residents of Riverwood were once again in an uproar, declaring there was a serial killer on the loose among them, demanding the sheriff do something to find the killer or killers, and do it now! Doors not usually locked suddenly made extra work for the locksmith due to increased demands in orders for sturdier locks to be installed. Mothers walked children to and from school with containers of mace in their hands. Teenagers no longer attended nighttime submarine races with steam covered car windows parked overlooking the lake. Fathers made sure guns were loaded and handy. Restaurants and stores usually open until dark closed while it was still daylight. Bars remained open but with additional armed security guards patrolling parking lots. To put it mildly, Riverwood businesses shut down with only those such as the grocery store, post office and gas stations remaining open during reduced daylight hours: the exception being bars. The already tense situation became worse. Newspapers and TV stations based out of Portland began nonstop reporting on both the murders of Jude and Grace. Tourism in Rockwood, what little there was this late in the season, stopped altogether. The only person who appeared cool, calm, and collected was one man.

"I'm sure glad I didn't get around to registering the sale of Grace's condo or drawing up a contract making her partner in the business. There would be no way I could explain those transactions," Melvin muttered. "All I need to do is prepare a bill of sale with her name on it, forge her signature, file with the court, and collect about half the sale price from her estate. Best of all, I'm in the clear for Jude's murder and the sheriff can't pin Gracie's death on me." Although this is what Melvin said to himself, he was not totally sure he was in the clear. Something lurking in his subconscious him made think he may have been observed dumping his nephew's body into that footer along with the Grace's body into the lake.

The drifter who had seen Melvin the night he unloaded Jude's body from his SUV trunk and dumped it in the footer wandered on to set up camp beside the lake. He thought nobody would believe him if he came forward to tell authorities in Portland what he observed when the local sheriff did not take him seriously. This added to his decision to move on until he arrived at the enticing shore of Mirror Lake. Liking what he saw, he decided to set up camp and do some fishing for a few days before heading elsewhere.

Melvin Prendergast, even if not especially liked or well thought of, was one of the town's leading citizens due to his wealth. The drifter, David Mercer, was a former Marine suffering from bouts of PTSD and alcoholism who took to wandering to deal with his war-related and wife desertion problems. No wonder the sheriff dismissed his story. The lack of a campfire and his dark grey/green colored tent in the moonless night made his presence unseen to the drunken figure half carrying half dragging what appeared to be a body to the deep end of the lake. Already three sheets to the wind, the result of drinking rot gut whiskey that fateful night, David gave thought to calling out to ask what the man was doing but thought better of it. "The guy could have gun. I'm sure the person he's dragging is already dead or it could be just trash. It would be best not to see or hear anything, or I could end up dead like the guys next to me in those foxholes, so don't get involved any further," he quietly slurred. To ease his mind, he drained the last few swallows of cheap whiskey from the bottle he was holding before laying it aside quietly to avoid detection.

Melvin, barely sober, tied a can of unused paint found in a closet around Grace's waist. He used the bulky bathrobe belt in a feeble effort to secure it and send her beneath the lake surface and keep her body there. This would have worked if the bulk of the bathrobe belt had not pulled loose when caught in underwater weeds sending it and the paint can to the lake bottom. This allowed her bloated body to float to the surface three days later where it was spotted by two local fishermen.

Melvin and Betty attended funeral services held for Grace. Melvin sent the largest basket of flowers of any mourners. He kept wiping his eyes and repeatedly honking his bulbous nose into a large white linen handkerchief to the point that his display grief caused Betty to lean over and comment, "I didn't know you cared so much about her." Her words caused Melvin to cry harder. He shook his head but had nothing to say. He would have plenty to say later when, misty eyed, he would tell anyone willing to listen what a good secretary she had been and how much he would miss her. Unfortunately for Melvin, his grief would produce nightmares so vivid he would awaken screaming the names of Grace and Jude, to the astonishment of Betty. This nightly ritual became extremely distressing to Betty, so much so when Melvin refused to seek psychiatric help, she kicked him out of their bedroom, then the house. She soon filed for divorce. She ended up receiving what she believed to be more than half of everything Melvin owned without any objection on his part. He made the unfortunate decision to move into what had been Grace's condo at Betty's urging just for spite.

Finding himself living alone there two months later, Melvin took his life with a bullet to the head after ingesting a quart of gin in less than an hour. There were no calling hours. Only five people attended his graveside funeral. They were Sharon Murphy, two of her closest minions, the preacher and the mortician who would not have been there if not needed to drive the hearse to and from the cemetery. Ex-wife Betty did not attend. There were no flowers beyond a meager, casket-top spray of white carnations and fern provided by the church memorial fund, attested to by Sharon, along with providing the rumor Melvin's death was no suicide. She started the rumor he was murdered by the killer or killers who took the lives of Jude and Grace. Once again, Riverwood became the focus of unwelcome news media with attention extending to Seattle. This served to fan fears among local citizens so intensely they began suspecting each other of committing the murders.

CHAPTER THIRTEEN

Cindy was having second thoughts about opening the knitting store in the rundown section of Riverwood. Bad publicity surrounding two murders, in addition to what the coroner deemed Melvin's suicide, along with approaching winter made it seem like a bad idea, at least for now. It didn't help when remembering Josh said he would assist should she decided to carry out those plans, and they had fallen in love despite all the ugly rumors. It was painful knowing they would never become a happily married couple due to his death. She was not looking forward to spending another lonely winter in the house she once shared with deceased husband Harold, or her new-found love Josh. Even though she sold many of the momentous and artwork at the church yard sale, and put smiling pictures of Harold away, everywhere she looked reminded her of him and the wonderful life they shared before leukemia took him. Josh's suicide only added to her feelings of depression now that she was aware of why he had taken such drastic action.

"I have got to find something useful to do," Cindy expressed to Ellie Montgomery when they sat talking over a rare lunch Cindy decided to indulge in at the local deli just a month before Josh died. "Gardening is done for another year, along with the flowers. I can't just sit out there and twiddle my thumbs or knit all winter, or I'll go stark raving mad!"

Cindy's revelation gave Ellie an idea. "Why don't you sign on to volunteer at the hospital?" she suggested. "I can always use another volunteer. The pink uniforms the ladies wear can be very sexy, especially when worn by someone built like you," continued Ellie as she dug with gusto into her chicken fried steak and mashed potatoes.

"I'm not interested in looking sexy," Cindy replied. At the time she was not particularly interested in having lunch with Ellie either, but the woman joined her without an invitation. Cindy did not want to seem unfriendly, so said nothing, acting as if she was happy to have company when Ellie plopped down on the empty booth seat across from her.

"I can always order a couple of uniforms in a size too large," replied Ellie through a mouthful of food. "Come on, Cindy! We need more volunteers in preparation for the new wing opening looming closer, and you would be perfect. You don't have any family responsibilities . . ." Seeing the look of pain cross Cindy's face, Ellie almost felt sorry she had added the insensitive statement to her conversation. She was aware Cindy and Harold were trying to have a child, and that did not happen. She also knew Cindy was seeing Josh Morgan on a regular basis, a relationship she did not want to see getting more serious. Ellie was having designs on the handsome and successful man herself, even though stonewalled by him in the face of what he considered her overly aggressive and suggestive flirting.

Ellie had the gut feeling if Cindy became involved as a member of the hospital volunteer program, she would not have energy to spend as much time with Josh. Thus, she would make sure this would happen due to the fact she oversaw the volunteer program with authority to assign working hours and days for all volunteers. This sense of power and knowing Cindy was a person who could not say no to a worthwhile project to which she was committed, would give Ellie the opportunity to limit time Cindy would have to spend with Josh.

After spending over an hour listening to Ellie's harangue through dessert, Cindy agreed to sign on as a hospital volunteer. She was not aware of Ellie's plan to become available to Josh when he would find himself alone most evenings. Ellie felt confident she would find a way to interject herself into his life by offering a sympathetic ear, a few unsavory rumors involving Cindy and offering her body to comfort him in those lonely hours when Cindy would be on duty. "It's great you are volunteering," Ellie gushed. "You will need to attend training classes for a month. They are held six evenings a week from six until ten p.m. Monday through Saturday. We meet in the hospital cafeteria, so you won't have to fix dinner. Meals are a free perk since no salary is involved."

"Why do you meet on Friday and Saturday evenings?" Cindy inquired. "Most people have plans for weekends, me included now that Josh and I are steadily dating." Ellie realized she had had to come up with an immediate answer. Training classes did not currently include weekend evenings until just this moment. "We needed to hurry up the program by adding weekend evening sessions in order to be ready for the opening of the new wing," became her glib response. "That's only four weekends so it's no big deal. Surely you can sacrifice four weekend evenings with Josh for such a good cause."

"I suppose you are right," answered Cindy thoughtfully.

You bet I am right, thought Ellie. "I'll make sure to order your uniforms two sizes too large," she added, barely able to suppress a smile while gathering her coat and purse to leave. "I've got to go. You promise you will be there tomorrow evening at six?"

"I didn't realize training sessions started so soon," replied Cindy. "Josh and I have plans for dinner, but since I agreed to become a hospital volunteer, I will be there."

"That's my girl." *I knew you would not back out once you committed*, Ellie gleefully thought. "I'm sure Josh will understand when you call to let him know you won't be available for those next few weekends and why." At the same time, Ellie was trying to think of three or four gullible people to contact who would start the training program tomorrow evening on short notice.

"But . . . my uniforms haven't even been ordered yet," Cindy stammered.

"Not to worry. Everyone will be wearing street clothing until the uniforms arrive," Ellie assured her. "Now I really must go," she announced again, scooting completely out of the booth.

"See you tomorrow evening at the training session?" asked Cindy.

"I won't be there. Laura Scott teaches the sessions. I only attend now and then since I'm the director of the program and I have plans. I know you will like Laura." That said, she walked out of the restaurant and left Cindy to pick up the tab for both lunches.

Ellie, distracted by thinking of how to approach Laura and find several people to attend weekend training session sprinted out the restaurant door with no thought of paying for her meal. Cindy remained seated and tried to place Laura Scott. Then it suddenly came to her. Laura Scott was one of Sharon Murphy's closest minions! "Oh dear, what have I agreed to? But I can't let Ellie down. I'm sure Josh will understand when I tell him why we won't be having evening dinners six days a week for the next month." Cindy was unaware there would be more than just a few evenings they would not be sharing dinners after training completed. "If I had known what Ellie was up to back then, Josh and I would still be together," she lamented as memories came flooding back.

On the fateful day Cindy agreed to become a volunteer, as soon as Ellie got into her car, she reached for her cell phone and pressed the button for a familiar number. It rang twice. "Hello. What do you want and make it quick?" demanded Sharon Murphy.

"Hi Sharon. It's Ellie."

"Do you think I can't read the name on my cell phone alerting me to who is calling?" she snapped.

"Sounds like you need more Ativan for your nerves, Sharon," replied Ellie, her voice dripping with concern.

"Damn right! What do you want this time? If you didn't have contacts I need, I would tell you where to go!" snarled Sharon. Ellie winced but continued. "I need three or four volunteers to show up starting tomorrow evening for a month of hospital volunteer training, including Friday and Saturday evenings. The classes run from six until ten p.m., along with Laura Scott as the instructor. They need not continue as volunteers after the training program is finished. In fact, it would be better if they did not continue as volunteers." She knew being short on volunteers would provide even more reasons for a dedicated Cindy to work extra hours.

"Can do, but it will cost you more little magic mood elevators and spending money. You sure you only want three or four people? I have enough dirt on certain people to supply ten or more ladies who wouldn't want their peccadillos broadcast to the world should they decline the opportunity to do as they are told."

"Three or four will be enough," replied Ellie. "I don't want too many so one of them can be assigned a lot of extra evening work once the hospital wing opens should they decide to continue volunteering."

Sharon started to laugh, emitting the sound of a braying donkey. "Who's the lucky girl who gets those extra hours? It wouldn't be Cindy Marsh, would it? I know you've got the hots for Josh Morgan, and that would provide a convenient way to get Cindy away from Josh. I must admit you have a lot of balls to pull off a stunt like this," Sharon cackled.

"And how would you know the lucky woman is Cindy?" asked Ellie. "I just talked her into becoming a volunteer not more than five minutes ago."

"That's for me to know and you not to find out," replied Sharon. "I have eyes and ears everywhere in this town, county and beyond. Consider yourself lucky we are friends since you are such a slut! I could have a field day spreading rumors about you with your appetite for men. Do we have a deal for Ativan and some spending money in the range of one hundred dollars?"

Ellie blanched when Sharon mentioned her sexual appetites. She knew full well Sharon had the ability to ruin her plans and reputation. "We have a deal, but I may have trouble getting the meds, but the pharmacist owes me a favor."

Sharon gave a dirty laugh. "Just screw his brains out like you always do and he will give you whatever you want. I will expect payment in full by five p.m. Leave it at the same location." She hung up without saying goodbye.

One of these days I am going to throttle that old bag, thought Ellie, *but not until I have no further use for her. Only God knows when that will be until I can find someone willing to do my bidding for a hundred bucks, an occasional meal, and a few pills while I pretend to be her friend so everyone in this town thinks I am being charitable associating with the likes of Sharon Murphy. At least it's a perk to be on her good side, or I would be run out of town on a rail for seducing more than half the upstanding male citizens calling Riverwood home. What does it matter if I have a high libido? Does that make me a slut? If I am a slut, what does it make the men who have sex with me?*

Ellie Montgomery could be considered attractive in that she could be soft spoken, even overly sympathetic, when interacting with hospital patients or listening to people in general while they unloaded their troubles. Her voluptuous build and provocative lips caught the attention of men, even though her facial features were average. Her eyes bore a feline quality the color of straw, causing curious stares, something she became aware of early in life. Those eyes did not stop her from making it known to local boys and men she had a very high libido. By age fourteen she had seduced the entire football team of the high school they all attended, along with the assistant principal. By age sixteen she had undergone two abortions, paid for by leading citizens of Rockwood, both done without the knowledge of her parents. She left home at age eighteen and enrolled in nursing school provided by a teaching hospital located in Portland. It did not take long before she knew the brand name and color of underwear worn by interns and several doctors, while still able to keep her nursing instructors and fellow students in the dark regarding associated activities providing such information.

Returning to Riverwood following graduation, Ellie adopted the persona of what everyone believed was an angel of mercy. But those in the know were carefully chosen as upstanding male members of society who did not want their indiscretions known to their significant others or the public. Ellie was sure she would have Josh Morgan's notch on her belt, if not his name and hers on a marriage license before the end of the month, two months at the latest. Approaching forty, Ellie knew it was time to settle down before her allure faded entirely. At the same time, she wanted a hunk of a sexy man with money to settle down with permanently. Josh Morgan met her check list, even if he was six years her junior. *The age difference between us makes it more than likely I'll be alone for less time when we grow old. That, and I happen to believe in the adage; you get 'em young and raise 'em the way you want 'em!*

Josh was disappointed to learn dinners were called off with Cindy, especially Friday and Saturday nights for the next month, but said he understood when she told him why.

"It's only a month. After the training classes are finished it will be only a few hours a day or a rare evening or weekend," Cindy told him. But what she said did not lessen his sadness at not being with her to brighten shared evenings after a hard day on the job; even though she routinely sent him home at a decent hour without engaging in sex to avoid possible pregnancy before marriage and more rumors.

"What am I going to do when my job is finished here," he wondered aloud while alone and pacing aimlessly around the living room of what had been the house. "Even if I continue to live here, I will have to be away from time to time for work, unless I can come up with some type of work to keep me here." The thought of buying vacant land around Mirror Lake and building a golf course came to his mind. "I've got enough money to buy land and contacts with people who can afford to invest in such a venture. It would provide a regular source of income, and with me being the manager, I can ask Cindy to be my wife," he whispered to himself. The thought of holding her in his arms to make love every night and waking up beside her every morning sent chills up his spine. His thoughts were interrupted by ringing of the house phone. He was tempted to not answer. Curiosity got the better of him when it kept on with persistent ringing.

"Hello, Josh Morgan speaking."

"Mr. Morgan, my name is David. You don't know me, but I know you are the architect and consultant overseeing the building of the new hospital wing. Do you have time to talk?"

"We can continue this conversation when you tell me your last name and what you want," replied Josh warily.

"Last names aren't important for what I want you to know," replied David.

"Exactly what do you want me to know?" Josh asked.

"I was witness to a body being dumped in the hospital wing footer," replied David. "The same man, driving the same SUV bearing the same license plate number, also threw that woman into the lake—the woman who was later reported to have been murdered."

Although this information sent chills up the back of his neck, Josh responded, "Why are you calling me, and why I'm supposed to believe someone who refuses to give me their last name?"

"I can give you the make, model, color, and license plate numbers of the SUV the man was driving, along with a description of him and what he was wearing. I'm calling you because you're in charge of the building project and enjoy a believable reputation," came David's reply.

"If you have this kind of information, why don't you contact the sheriff? I'm sure he would be very interested in what you have to say, not to mention you could collect the posted reward money when this person is apprehended and brought to justice," remarked Josh.

"I'm a homeless drifter suffering from what I now believe to be PTSD. I tried telling the sheriff, but he blew me off when I told him I could describe the man dumping what turned out to be that Prichart guy's body in the footer and that woman, Grace, in the lake. I am not interested in reward money. I get disability checks," countered David.

"If that is the case, what makes you think I would believe you when the sheriff didn't believe you?"

"Because you served in the marines, just like I did, and we are supposed to look out for each other and do the honorable thing," replied the caller. Having served in the Marines, this statement got Josh's immediate attention. "Where did you serve?" he asked. There was no response, and the phone line went dead before Josh could ask the caller how he knew he had served in the Marines. Josh was left with the feeling he was being taken for a fool by some deranged individual who got his kicks out of making prank phone calls.

At the time of the call, Josh didn't have any idea David Mercer hung up because he was having a flashback to the time seven of his buddies were killed in an foxhole, him the lone survivor while serving in Afghanistan; or that he had been captured and endured two years as a POW at the hands of the Taliban before escaping barely alive after numerous brutal beatings and lack of food, or making his way on foot to a M.A.S.H. unit before being evacuated for a few days of observation in a German hospital. After a week of rest and nutritious food, doctors there determined he was not severely physically harmed enough to remain hospitalized in Germany and would be better served if he was sent home with an honorable discharge. On their recommendation, he was sent home to America with an honorable discharge to find an empty house, learn his father had died, find his car and wife gone along with money in a shared bank account, and nobody willing to give him a job. He did finally manage to find a job as a farmhand. He sought treatment with the VA for what he described as lost time, in addition to an amplified reaction to loud noise and nightmares where he believed he was back on the front line or being held captive. He was given a prescription for a month's supply of anti-anxiety medication and sent on his way.

This is when David decided to spend his mustering out pay for camping supplies and a bicycle before hitting the road despite pleas from a farm manager to stay and work the farm. How he ended up going from a farm in Kansas to end up in Riverwood, Oregon, he had no idea as the days, weeks and months went by. He spent most of his time focused on finding shelter beyond his small tent, a change of dry but not always clean clothing, and food after MRE rations purchased from the PX ran out. Had it not been for his trusty .38 and being a crack shot killing squirrels, quail, and rabbits to roast over open campfires, he would have gone hungry after the first two months on his quest to nowhere in particular. Large cities and their associated noises, along with large numbers of people, led him to avoid spending time there. He preferred small towns like Riverwood that rolled up their streets at dusk. In this type of setting, he became an expert dumpster diver when faced with gnawing hunger before seeking a quiet place to set up camp and do occasional odd jobs for however long a time suited him, or as in many cases, was encouraged to move on by the local sheriff or police. Before witnessing disposal of two bodies, David Mercer was a man without a mission beyond survival. That changed after what he witnessed. He started to focus on finding someone who believed his story and ways to expose the perpetrator. Then residents of Riverwood could get back to lives once considered normal without fear of a possible serial killer living in their midst. Being a drifter, this goal proved difficult.

CHAPTER FOURTEEN

Betty Prendergast Stevens married a local bartender one month after Melvin killed himself. Talk about rumors when this became known! Despite rumors involving Betty and her new husband, she was irate upon learning Melvin had a second and more recent will drawn up, naming Cindy Marsh beneficiary of billions of dollars to build a new entertainment complex, including the stipulation she build a restaurant named Gracie's.

"Rumors concerning those two must have been true; he was sleeping with Cindy and Grace! Sleeping with Grace I understand since they spent a lot of time together, but I can't even begin to understand Melvin's connection to Cindy! Why would he change the will and name her to build a resort? Just look at what I found here where Grace was living!" Betty was beside herself with anger while she verbally unloaded on Ellie, who accompanied her to inspect the condo. "I should have listened to Sharon Murphy!" Betty declared as she started clearing out what had been Grace's personal items from the condo; items including a pair of Melvin's undershorts found under the master bedroom bed, two complete changes of his clothing hanging in the closet and a bottle of Viagra with his name on the prescription container sitting on a shelf in the master bathroom medicine cabinet.

"When I went to question that slut Cindy Marsh, she would not open the door to her house when she saw me standing on the porch! I know she was home! I will contest the new will!" Betty angrily declared. "Melvin had no right to change the will after all the years I put up with that pompous ass, his bullshit and womanizing! Now I know I didn't even begin to get half of our assets! I should have gotten everything!"

Egged on by her dubious friend Ellie Montgomery to hire an attorney she knew, Betty hired Edward Walter Williams, Esquire, based out of Seattle but willing to take on cases anywhere a computer could be accessed whether licensed in that jurisdiction or not. Betty had no idea Ellie would receive a finder's fee for the referral, nor did she know the skanky reputation of the attorney, or she might have been more cautious. Blindsided by anger and pure greed, Betty would have hired the devil if she thought he could invalidate Melvin's new will and get her hands on billions of dollars and land, allowing her to live in the lap of luxury for the remainder of her and her new husband's life together.

With the finder's fee pittance of three hundred dollars from her attorney friend, paid in cash, Ellie elected to purchase new, sexy, black lace underwear, including a black garter belt. "Nothing turns a man on faster than lacy, crotchless, black panties, a matching bra, and especially a garter belt and black silk stockings on legs like mine while wearing red high heels," she convinced herself. The problem would be how to persuade straight-shooting Josh Morgan to see her dressed in those items when he obviously had eyes only for Cindy Marsh. "I don't know what that man sees in her," said Ellie to her reflection in the bathroom mirror while modeling her purchases. "But I aim to find out and use it against her. I know she can be attractive in a sort of country girl way when she fixes her hair and puts on a little makeup, but she doesn't hold a candle to my looks when I get dressed up to go on the hunt."

What Ellie did not understand was Cindy did not feel the need to go on the hunt. She was an upfront, honest person who could look you straight in the eye, and if she said she was going to do something, she did it without expecting compensation or praise. What Ellie looked upon as weakness, ninety-seven percent of other people who knew Cindy saw as strength of character; everyone but Sharon Murphy and three percent of her rumor-hungry friends hellbent upon destroying Cindy's reputation to preserve their reputations and sense of power.

It did not take long before Ellie recognized the answer to her prayers. A handsome but battered drifter was admitted to the hospital following a severe beating by a gang of misfit drug dealers while camping beside Mirror Lake. A condo resident decided to take a walk along the lake and found the man dazed and bleeding while muttering something about needing to get his buddies behind enemy lines. The man called Sheriff Heinz, who had him transported via ambulance to the hospital for what appeared to be a severe head injury in addition to multiple cuts, scrapes and bruises. That evening, Ellie, filling in for the regular nursing supervisor, approached Cindy to inform her she would be needed to sit beside the restrained drifter.

"You are just the person for this job," said Ellie. "You have a way of calming people down, and this guy needs your help. He is restrained, so you'll be in no danger. Besides, once we got the mud and blood washed away, his wounds stitched and bandaged in the ER, he isn't bad looking. I am hoping you convince him to give his name or someone to contact. As it stands now, all he does is babble. The doctors don't know anything about his medical history. Without a name and some knowledge about his medical history, there isn't much we can do besides calm him down, clean his wounds and feed him. How about it? Are you willing to play nursemaid a few more hours tonight? We are short on staffing, or I would ask one of the nurses to do private duty. I am confident I can find someone to relieve you before midnight."

Cindy, already tired from working double hours as a volunteer, sighed but agreed to lend a helping hand. She and Josh had plans for a late dinner date at his home after her volunteer hours were over at nine p.m. Those plans required cancellation when she agreed to Ellie's request.

Josh knew there was a problem when her name came up on his cell phone. "Don't tell me you are cancelling our date again? This is getting to be a habit! First it was a month of training classes. Those completed, now It seems you are needed for extra hours following your regular shift," he said before she started to speak.

Cindy attempted to explain. "I'm sorry, Josh, but we have a patient who needs a private nurse or at least someone to sit with him. Ellie requested I stay and try to calm him down. Doctors need to find out his name, or if he has someone they could call. She said she tried to find someone to stay with him but was unsuccessful. Scuttlebutt around the hospital says the man was badly beaten by more than one person while camping out by the lake. The sheriff seems to think it might be gang related. There have been reports of rival gangs growing pot in the wooded area southeast of town down by the far end of the lake. Please tell me you understand," she pleaded.

"I do understand, but will you be safe going to your car late at night? Would you like me to meet you when you are relieved of duty?" he asked. By the tense sound of his voice, she knew he was upset. "I will be fine. Hospital administration recently hired a security guard to walk night

146

shift staff to and from the parking lot. I'm sure he won't mind escorting me to my car. Ellie told me there will be someone to relieve me before he leaves. I want you to get some dinner and a good night's sleep. I will see you tomorrow for a quick lunch. I will find a way to make it up to you. I promise."

"I like the sound of that," said Josh. Cindy could picture him with a twinkle returning to his eyes and a sexy smile replacing a frown. "How about another chocolate cake or better yet, a nice long weekend together in Portland?" he offered in response to what she just said.

"Why, Josh Morgan! Are you trying to make me a tainted woman should I accept your offer of a long weekend out of town?" Cindy replied coyly.

No, I want to propose marriage, he thought. "You could never be a tainted woman in my eyes," he replied while gazing at the large diamond engagement ring he planned to give her.

"Never say never," came Cindy's playful answer, an answer she would later regret. "I've got to get going. Ellie is coming down the hall in my direction, and she does not look happy. Good night my dear. Sleep well. I love you," she whispered just before Ellie entered the hallway to stand beside her with a decided scowl on her face.

"Why aren't you sitting with the patient I told you about? He is raising holy hell and trying to get out of his restraints!

If he keeps this up, we are going to have to move patients from adjoining rooms and we don't have any empty rooms!"

Cindy closed her eyes briefly and bit her tongue at the harshness Ellie portrayed to prevent saying something she might later regret. "I'm sorry Ellie. I had to give Josh a call to let him know we won't be meeting for dinner," replied a weary Cindy. "Please tell me again, what is the room number of the patient? It has been a long day. I'm tired and don't remember."

Ellie immediately put on her understanding face. "I'm sorry I spoke harshly. I know you have worked double your volunteer hours already, but patients are complaining about the noise. He is in room 124, three rooms toward the end of the hall on the first floor. I'll have the cook whip up something for your dinner since you won't be meeting Josh. Would a hamburger with the works and a thick strawberry milkshake work?"

"That would be nice," said Cindy as she started walking in the direction of the elevator to the first floor.

Too bad I don't have any rat poison to put in that milkshake, thought Ellie as she watched Cindy disappear into the elevator. *That would get you out of the way faster than this game playing!*

The drifter was shouting at the top of his lungs when Cindy entered the room. "Get these damn restraints off my ankles and wrists!" he demanded. "I've got to help get my men get to safety! I can't do that while I'm tied down in this prison camp!"

"Sir, please calm down, Sir. You are in the hospital not prison. My name is Cindy Marsh. I will be sitting with you for a couple of hours. What's your name?"

The man glared at Cindy, his eyes full of suspicion. "I didn't know the Taliban used women to guard prisoners," he replied bitterly.

"I don't know what you mean. There are no Taliban here. You are in a hospital in Riverwood, Oregon, U.S.A." she answered. "Somebody, probably several men, beat you while you camped by Mirror Lake. You ended up here thanks to a good Samaritan calling the sheriff." At least now Cindy knew he was in the military somewhere in the Middle East. "Can you tell me your name, soldier?" she asked.

"I'm not telling you another damned thing and don't call me soldier! I already told your superiors my name, rank and serial number! Now untie me and give me some water! That's the rule according to the Geneva Convention. You are required to give me water! Don't bother bringing rat soup. I won't eat it!"

Cindy was trying her best to remain calm. "Sir, I'm not a Taliban guard. I am a pink lady volunteer here at the hospital in Riverwood, Oregon." She pointed to the pink uniform he chose to ignore. "The nursing supervisor asked me to sit with you. I will be glad to give you some water." She lifted the glass containing water and a straw to his lips. He took several sips then spit in her face.

"Sir, that was uncalled for!" said Cindy as she wiped water from her face with several small tissues taken from a box sitting on the bedside table. "I'm only here to help you."

"Some help you are!" he yelled. Cindy reached out and gently brushed back a stand of matted brown hair out of his eyes. "Don't touch me! You are nothing but a filthy whore!" he yelled, turning his head away from her.

"I am not a whore. I'm a pink lady volunteer here at the hospital," she replied again quietly. This time the drifter glanced at her face, something he had not done earlier. The contact was broken by a knock at the door. "Who is it?" asked Cindy.

"It's the cook with your burger and shake ma'am. Alright if I come in?"

"Of course, you can come in," replied Cindy graciously.

An unsmiling man dressed in a white shirt and pants covered with a grease-stained apron pushed open the door. "I hope you realize I only stayed after we closed the kitchen to please Ellie. I hope you don't plan to make this a habit!" He let go with this statement before he noticed who was wearing a pink volunteer uniform. "Sorry. I didn't realize you were still here Miss Cindy. I will be more than happy to fix anything you want. Just send the word. I think it's nice of you to spend time helping make this gentleman more comfortable." His change in attitude likely came about when he realized Cindy could mention his bad attitude to Ellie. He was aware Ellie could make his life miserable.

The drifter directed a hostile glare toward the cook when he placed the food tray on the bedside table, then turned to leave. After the door closed, the drifter turned attention back to Cindy as she picked up the hamburger and prepared to take a bite. "Don't eat that! It's probably made from boiled rat," he shouted.

Startled, Cindy lowered the burger away from her mouth. "Here, smell it. It smells like beef to me." She brought the sandwich up close to his nose. He would have batted it away if not for the restraints on both wrists. He sniffed the sandwich warily when Cindy moved it only inches away from his nose. "Smells like raw onion meant to cover the stink of rat," he replied wrinkling his nose.

"There is raw onion, lettuce, tomato, dill pickle and mustard on it. Want to try a bite?" she offered.

"You take a bite first," he countered. "If you don't gag, throw up or die within the next few minutes, I might try," he responded while focused skeptically on another covered container sitting on the tray. "What's in the plastic container? Rice water? That's about all we get to eat from these damn rag heads," he said in disgust.

"It's a strawberry milkshake," replied Cindy. "Have you seen anyone wearing a turban since you've been here?" When the drifter did not reply she asked again, an edge to her voice. "Well, have you seen anyone wearing a turban?" The drifter appeared to be thinking about an answer before he squinted his eyes. "No, but that doesn't mean they aren't around. They hide in the shadows."

Cindy took a big bite of the burger, chewed and swallowed then reached for the milkshake. "Are you sure you don't want a bite of the sandwich? It sure tastes like a medium cooked hamburger should taste." Without waiting for his answer, she lifted the burger to his lips. To her surprise he took a small bite. "That wasn't so bad, was it?" she asked. He didn't answer. "How about another bite? I was informed you haven't been eating." He nodded and took a larger bite. Cindy smiled with encouragement while unwrapping the straw and forcing it through the opening in the lid of the milkshake container. She took a sip. "Mmmm. Boy is this good! The cook must have used fresh strawberries. Would you like a taste?" The man shook h his head negatively.

"What I want is for you to take these damned restraints off me," he said raising his voice again.

"I am sorry, but I can't do that," said Cindy regretfully.

"Why not?" he asked with a slightly less venomous and almost pleading tone to his voice this time.

"You have been, how do I say this politely?" she mused before coming right out to say, "You have been raising hell to the point everyone thinks you could hurt them or yourself. You will have to show personal restraint before your doctor gives order for these to be removed." The drifter appeared to be contemplating her words but did not reply. To soften the moment, Cindy offered him a sip of the milkshake. He ended up draining most of the contents, closed his eyes, sighed, leaned back onto the pillow and began to snore.

Cindy finished what remained of the now cold burger followed by the few remaining sips of the shake. She was so tired she pulled her chair closer to the bed and lay her head down on the mattress above the patient's restrained right arm and soon drifted off. It wasn't long before Ellie quietly opened the door to room 124, tip toed inside to stand watching. An evil smile played across her lips as she thought, *Well now, isn't that a cozy little scene? I think I will have the security guard come and take a picture. I feel sure Josh would love to see the woman he views as a saint cozying up to a male patient.*

It was almost midnight when something awakened Cindy. She rubbed her eyes thinking she saw a flash of light but convinced herself she was dreaming. The drifter was still sound asleep when she gathered up her sweater and purse to leave after a glance at her watch to learn the hour was approaching midnight. She stopped by the nursing station to let the nurse know she was leaving and ask when someone was coming to relieve her at the drifter's bedside.

The night nurse gave her a look implying she did not know what Cindy was talking about. "I haven't been told there would be anyone to relieve you. The patient is in restraints. If he gets agitated again, I have orders to give him a shot of the powerful tranquilizer Thorazine. In fact, I am surprised he has been so quiet that I haven't needed to give him a dose already. Usually, by this time of night, he's yelling like a banshee about getting his men to safety. Personally, I think the poor man is having bouts of PTSD aggravated by the recent beating and head injury. I'm going to suggest Doctor Rainer should consider ordering a psych consult, along with bringing in a neurologist when he makes rounds early in the morning."

Cindy started to walk away. The nurse continued to walk beside her to begin chatting. "Thanks for staying with the patient. Having you with him has been a blessing to staff and surrounding patients. I hope you can see your way clear to be here tomorrow night. By the way, he didn't per chance give you his name, or someone we can contact, did he?"

"No, I did learn he was in the military where there were Taliban but not the branch of service or exact location where he served," replied Cindy. "Maybe he will give me this information if I'm asked to return tomorrow." Cindy thought she heard the nurse mutter something that sounded like, "I am insisting you come back" as they parted. Cindy continued walking toward what she believed to be the now deserted front lobby. She was surprised to see the security guard sitting in one of the chairs, one leg casually draped over the chair arm. Cindy glanced at her wristwatch again. "I thought you went off duty at the stroke of midnight and it's almost a quarter past twelve." She thought she detected a sly grin on his face when he said he would be delighted to walk her to her car. His demeanor was polite after he stood, so she passed his look off as something she imagined due to fatigue.

After driving home, Cindy could hardly wait to undress, get into a nightgown and fall into bed without brushing her teeth. She even neglected to check her cell phone messages before turning the ring tone off for the night, so she failed to respond to Josh's call asking if she was home safe.

While concerned he did not hear from Cindy, Josh's disappointment that they had not met for dinner prevailed. He decided to go to bed without trying to call her again. "I'll call again early in the morning," he muttered before falling asleep due to sheer exhaustion from a hard day's work at the hospital building site, but not before he briefly chided himself for not making more of an effort to speak with Cindy yet tonight.

Cindy awakened at five a.m. the following morning. Her first action was turning her cell phone ring tone on. Only then did she discover the missed message from Josh. "It's only five a.m. He won't be awake for another hour, so I'll make coffee before I call him and make plans," she muttered to herself. Before the coffee finished perking, her cell phone rang. It was Ellie begging her to come to the hospital immediately to sit with the drifter. "Please, please come in as soon as you can! Our star patient has gone off the deep end again," she pleaded. "He isn't calming down following a shot of Thorazine! You are the only one who can calm him down. Nurses are starting to panic. Patients are signing themselves out against medical advice because of the uproar he is causing!"

I don't need this, thought Cindy. "I was there past midnight last night and just woke up," she replied irritably. Why didn't you inform me or the night nurse there would not be anyone coming to relieve me last night?" she inquired, a decided edge to her voice.

Once again Ellie had to think fast. "I'm sure I mentioned it to the head nurse. She must have forgotten to tell the night nurse I was unable to find anyone to replace you, but no harm done. The drifter slept until about two hours ago before he awakened to start raving again. That alone proves you are the calming influence I thought you would be, so please come in as soon as you can."

"Hold on until I get a quick shower, dress and get there as fast as I can legally drive. And you better have the cook prepare something edible for my breakfast, including regular coffee, and have it ready no later than three minutes after I arrive," replied Cindy curtly.

Ellie breathed a sigh of relief. Her lies worked. The drifter was not creating a disturbance, nor were patients signing themselves out against medical advice. Her plan was working to keep Cindy and Josh apart. "By the time Cindy arrives at the hospital I'll tell her the Thorazine did its work and the drifter calmed down," Ellie said aloud while lying at home in her comfortable bed. With a smile she reached over to set her snooze alarm for another ten minutes. "I have time before I need to shower, have a cup of coffee, get dressed and make it to the hospital before she arrives. I am so glad Cindy is such a people please. She is playing right into my hands. I have no doubt everything will go my way where Josh is concerned."

Ellie stood waiting for less than two minutes outside of room 124, clipboard in hand, before Cindy arrived. "It's about time you showed up," she said with a fake smile. "I'm glad you are here and equally glad to let you know the medication has finally taken effect. But it will not last more than a few hours before the patient will awaken and cause more chaos when told he is going to be evaluated by a psychiatrist and neurologist. This is when you need to be here to calm him down. Of course, this will be in addition to your volunteer hours of eight a.m. until noon, allowing you time for a quick cafeteria lunch before you are needed with the drifter." Ellie could easily have allowed Cindy to take those morning hours off, but that would mean she would have the opportunity to have an early lunch with Josh, and she wasn't going to allow this to happen. "But Ellie, I'm not a trained nurse," objected Cindy. "I'm only a volunteer, and a new volunteer at that! Shouldn't someone with knowledge of how to deal with this type of patient sit with the drifter?" she asked. "Josh and I had plans for later this afternoon. He will be upset if I cancel our plans again."

"Don't you think I've tried to find someone?" replied Ellie curtly. The lie rolled off her lips as smoothly as expensive, ice-cold vodka going down her throat. "The drifter should only be here a few more days before we ship him off to an institution. I have people working around the clock trying to find which branch of service he was deployed after we managed to learn he was trying to protect his buddies in some fox hole located in Asia."

Thanks for not giving me any credit for that bit of information, thought Cindy.

"That, along with what you told the night nurse concerning him referring to the cook as a rag head who fed him only cooked rat and rice water. You did tell her that, didn't you?" Ellie's question caught Cindy off guard.

"I may have. I was so tired I don't remember what we talked about," she replied evasively. Her gut was telling her not to divulge what she and the drifter discussed. "Are you sure this is only going to take more than a few days?"

Ellie worked hard to contain a smile. "I'm sure. It may not take that long," she replied. *I am even more sure Josh is going to think twice about having a relationship with you when he sees the picture of you cuddling up to a male patient when he thinks all you do is pass ice water, arrange and distribute donated flowers and push a cart filled with old magazines from room to room.* "Now get in there after lunch and be ready to hold the drifter's hand if that's what it takes to keep him calm. I need to make rounds. I'm covering for the nursing director again today. I'll check in on you every so often to make sure you are alright. Look. Here comes the cook with your breakfast. I hope you like crispy bacon, eggs benedict and sour dough toast with strawberry jam. Just let him know if you prefer decaf or regular coffee. I didn't know your preference, or I would have ordered it for you, too."

Ellie, you have the mind of a pea, thought Cindy. *I told you regular coffee!* "We've eaten enough meals together you know I drink regular coffee. In fact, why don't you order this type of breakfast for the drifter and included a carafe of regular coffee in case he would like some, too."

"What do you think this place is, a five-star restaurant?" snapped Ellie. "He will be served the same meal as other patients are being served on a regular diet. Feel free to share your breakfast with him like you shared your dinner with him last night."

Her comment concerning Cindy sharing her evening meal with the drifter gave a reason for her to wonder how Ellie knew this had taken place. Ellie had not been in the patient's room during the time food was there. "How do you know I shared my dinner with him?" questioned Cindy.

"Ha! Do you think Sharon Murphy has dibs on who has eyes and ears everywhere? She doesn't begin to hold a candle to my sources, so you need to make sure you behave yourself!" That said, Ellie walked away only to turn back adding, "You will be available until we find other arrangements for the drifter, won't you?" While delivered as a question it sounded more like an order. "You could hurry up the process by finding a way to convince him to give you a name. Should you be able to, I would be willing to name you volunteer of the year."

Cindy only nodded and opened the door to room 124 to find the drifter sleeping peacefully. This scene, added to other comments Ellie made, left Cindy wondering what she meant by telling her to behave herself.

It took three days, including evenings of eating and sharing meals with him, before the drifter started telling Cindy about himself, including his name, David Mercer. He served in the marines, lost seven buddies and was the lone survivor when their unit was struck by enemy fire. That was followed by time spent as a POW and a harrowing escape from his captors. While sympathetic to David's story, and making a promise to keep their conversations private, Cindy knew she had to tell the sheriff when David revealed he witnessed a man dragging what appeared to be a body and rolled it into one of the hospital construction footers before concrete was poured. He said he saw the same man driving the same SUV bearing the same license plate numbers and tossing what later turned out to be Grace's body into the lake. While she did not hold a law degree, Cindy knew withholding this type of information from authorities could cause her serious problems if or when David came forward with this information, especially if the sheriff had reason to believe she knew and had not informed him. At the time

Cindy was unaware David already approached the sheriff and was not believed.

As soon as she could, Cindy excused herself to go inform the nursing staff of David's name and what he told her concerning time served in the Marines, minus the sighting of who could be a cold-blooded killer disposing of bodies. Her next course of action was to phone Josh then Sheriff Heinz. She wanted Josh to be with her when she related details regarding a possible murder suspect when the sheriff arrived. Her call went to Josh's voice mail. "Josh, it's me, Cindy. I know you are not happy with me right now because I am spending so much time at the hospital, but we need to talk. Sorry I missed your call last night. Call me a soon as possible. I'm at the hospital early at Ellie's request. It is very important we talk." Josh waited an hour before returning her call, most of the time spent looking at the eight by ten glossy print someone slipped under his door during the night. He could not believe the image of Cindy with her head resting on the bed of a male patient. When he finally made the call, Cindy, noting who the caller was, excused herself from David's bedside and stepped out into the hall before for answering. She didn't want him hearing their conversation.

Josh interrupted her before she could speak beyond saying hello. "This is Josh. I'm the guy you have been dating until sitting with a male patient took priority. Yes, Cindy, we do need to talk but not on the phone. If you can manage to pry yourself loose long enough from the male patient you have been babysitting, I'll be waiting for you in the lobby when you finish your shift." He hung up before she could respond. *I wonder what is eating him,* thought Cindy. *He sounds like he has indigestion, or he is angry about something more than us missing a few dinners together.* She was unaware he was in the hospital lobby at the time of his call.

When she returned to David's room, he asked if she was upset over what he had told her. "I know I've been a total ass these past few days, and I'm sorry. I don't know what gets inside my head. Sometimes it feels like I am back in that foxhole watching my buddies being riddled with bullets, and I can't do anything to help them. Or I'm back in that hellhole of a prison eating disgusting rat meat to have strength enough to survive beatings and abuse." He was not able to tell her about a missing wife in Kansas following his discharge. He later divulged information about the missing car and bank account when he returned home from the service with an honorable discharge.

"I respect what you went through, and I am the one who is sorry. I am not upset with you," said Cindy, "Although I'm not a psychiatrist or nurse, I strongly suspect you are suffering from PTSD that is aggravated by the beating, and so does your attending doctor. That is why you will be seen by two more doctors, a psychiatrist and neurologist today after lunch. They specialize in helping patients like you recover." She could not help noticing the dark scowl spreading across David's face as she continued. "Please don't be upset when they come to speak with you and run some tests," cautioned Cindy. "I don't want you to end up in restraints again when you have been doing so well the past few days." Instead of the expected outburst, she was relieved when David responded softly. "Will you stay with me during those exams? You are the one person who understands what is going on inside my head. I tried getting help through the VA. All the VA did was prescribe an antidepressant that made me feel and act like a total zombie, so I stopped taking it, continued drinking and hit the road."

"If the doctors will allow it, I will be here with you," replied Cindy.

"They will allow you to stay in the room or they can go straight to hell!" shouted David.

"Shhhh. Stop talking so loudly or you will find yourself back in restraints," cautioned Cindy as she reached out to straighten his rumpled sheet. The last thing she expected was David to sit up and throw his arms around her neck any more than expecting Josh to walk into the room carrying a manila envelope in his right hand.

There was no doubt Josh was enraged. "It appears Ellie was right about you! You are a slut! Have you no shame when it comes to cavorting with a patient?" said Josh through clinched teeth.

Startled, Cindy removed David's arms from around her neck and helped him settle back on his pillow. "I can explain," she offered turning to face Josh.

"You can explain this current disgusting display of affection in addition to explaining this picture!" Josh angrily replied as he tossed the envelope onto the foot of David's bed. With shaking hands, Cindy picked up the envelope and opened it to find the picture taken by the security guard. Of course, she had no idea that Ellie Montgomery set that up the night Cindy briefly fell asleep with her head lying on edge of David's bed. Cindy was so dumbstruck she could not speak.

"I don't know who you are, but you have this situation all wrong mister," insisted David after glancing at the picture. "I was upset. Cindy was only trying to offer words of comfort when you walked in just now. I am guilty of hugging her, but it was purely out of gratitude for the way she has been helping me. How dare you call this angel of mercy a slut! If she dozed off with her head on my bed it was because it was late, and she was totally exhausted. If I had the strength, I would get out of this bed and make you and the person who took this picture sorry! How can you say such a terrible thing about this woman!" David felt the need to shout because Josh was already walking toward the door, leaving a very distraught Cindy holding the incriminating picture, along with knowledge it had to have been Ellie who deliberately set her up in order to obtain the picture. Now she understood. Ellie was the only one to benefit from the picture!

CHAPTER FIFTEEN

The following morning, after reviewing psychiatry and neurology reports, the attending doctor released David Mercer. This took place after he promised to move into a halfway house near the old downtown Riverwood area and continue twice weekly sessions with a psychiatrist. That same afternoon, with a heavy heart, Cindy returned to the hospital to turn in her pink volunteer uniforms inside Ellie's office. She could have pitched them into the laundry hamper sitting outside Ellie's office door, but Cindy wanted to make sure Ellie knew why she was not going to continue as a volunteer.

When Ellie had the gall to ask why she was resigning, Cindy let her have it. "You set me up so you could have a shot with Josh, you traitor! I thought you were my friend, but obviously not! How could you have arranged for that picture to be taken? You were aware I worked twelve straight hours each of the previous three days as a favor to you. You knew exactly what you were doing! And Josh thinks I'm the slut? I think that's backwards!"

Ellie shrugged her shoulders. "All's fair in love and war," she responded. "Before you hear it through the rumor mill, Josh and I are having a very private dinner at his house tonight. I expect a whole lot more to follow. I don't happen to be the prig you are when it comes to having sex. Don't bother wasting your time responding. Toss your uniforms in the hamper on your way out, or I will call security and have you thrown out!"

Cindy believed it would serve no useful purpose to continue meaningful dialogue. Ellie had shown her true colors. "Just remember what goes around comes around, Ellie," replied Cindy. Ellie just laughed and pointed toward the door instead of responding to her comment.

Security guard Gilbert Strong was waiting for Cindy at the front exit door. He wanted to plead his case when she approached to leave the hospital. "I can't tell you how sorry I am I took that picture. Ellie paid me a hundred bucks to take it. She said if I didn't take it, she would make sure I was fired. I need the money and job. My wife is pregnant. Ellie also said she would tell her I was cheating if I didn't do what she wanted," he explained with downcast eyes.

"I understand, Gilbert. No hard feelings. Don't worry about it. If Josh continues to refuse to give me an opportunity to explain, he is not the man I thought he was, and Ellie can have him. Tell your wife congratulations and hello for me."

After putting on a brave face for the encounter with the security guard, Cindy burst into tears by the time she made it through the lobby double glass doors and walked across the parking lot to unlock her truck door. She got in, and with her head leaning against the steering wheel, she began to sob in earnest. It took five minutes before she could get her emotions under control enough to drive home.

The next few weeks were not easy for Cindy. She found herself walking aimlessly throughout the house and in tears when she least expected them. Even after the weather turned bitter cold three weeks later, she bundled up in one of Harold's old hunting jackets, tied a scarf around her hair (in need of shampooing), and tossed a fishing line into the lake only to release any fish caught. She was not sleeping or eating properly. Within a month after the breakup, she had lost twenty pounds she did not need to lose. Meanwhile, Josh was taking advantage of Ellie's undivided attention, sympathy and proclivity for unrestrained sexual adventures. He found himself so enamored that he began to have thoughts of asking her to marry him.

Those thoughts changed when painful symptoms sent him to visit the local urologist. After an exam and blood test results came distressing information imparted by the doctor who did not look at him while conveying a diagnosis. "Josh, my friend, I hate to tell you, but you have a social disease called syphilis. I am sure you have heard the name before and how it can cause devastating effects to your brain, eyes and neurological system if left untreated." The horror on

Josh's face was unmistakable, prompting the doctor to continue. "Do not panic. It can be treated successfully, but you need to disclose the name or names of anyone you have been in contact with sexually. I am required by law to file a report containing those names to the county health department so they can contact that person or persons and have them seek treatment," said Dr. Simeon.

Stunned by the news, Josh continued to sit in silence for a full minute before he found his voice. Familiar with this type of reaction, Dr. Simeon waited patiently. "Can't this be problem be managed between you and me without involving the health department?" Josh asked.

The doctor shook his head. "Sorry Josh. No can do. If word got out, I could lose my license to practice medicine if I fail to report these findings. It is urgent to inform the person or persons with whom you have had sexual contact so they can get treatment. We do not need a full-blown epidemic of syphilis in Riverwood. If, per chance, a woman becomes pregnant and her husband or lover had intercourse with the person who infected you, the pregnant woman's unborn child could suffer sever health effects, including blindness at the very least. The bottom line is, I need the name or names immediately for my report."

Josh hung his head in shame. "There has been only one person, Ellie Montgomery."

"Are you sure? I've heard rumors you have a sexual relationship with Cindy Marsh."

"We do not have sex. Cindy said she wasn't ready for that yet," replied Josh. *But she was ready to play footsies with a male hospital patient or patients*, he thought angrily.

"Josh, you need to get up from the cart, drop your pants and bend over. I'm going to give you a shot of long-acting penicillin in the butt. You need to return in a month for another shot just in case a few spirochetes manage to survive this injection. In the meantime, have absolutely no sex until you get a clean bill of health from me. Go home, take a shower, wash your underwear and linens with bleach added to the wash cycle and be glad we caught this early."

Josh had barely pulled up his shorts and pants in preparation to leave the examination room when the urologist called for his nurse to come to an adjoining exam room and inject him, the doctor, with a dose of penicillin. When she asked the doctor why he needed penicillin, he said he was coming down with a cold. But in fact, the doctor had spent several hours with Ellie two afternoons before. Most of that time was not spent in conversation!

Josh was embarrassed facing the receptionist as he paid his insurance co-pay. From the look on her face, he had the feeling it would not take long before more than half the town's residents would be aware he had a sexually transmitted disease and where he acquired it. He debated whether to call Ellie or let the health department do the dirty work. By the time he drove home, he decided he should be the one to make the call so she would not be blindsided by such news from the health department. "At least I owe her that much," he muttered.

Instead of being grateful, Ellie was livid upon hearing the news. "I infected you with syphilis?" she bellowed. "It wasn't me! It had to have been Cindy Marsh! How dare you accuse me?" She ended the call before Josh could let her know she should expect a call from the health department and that he had not had sexual contact with Cindy.

"How could I have been so stupid to let this happen?" he chided himself. He would chide himself more harshly a few hours later when his cell phone rang. The caller turned out to be Sharon Murphy. She asked to meet with him privately that evening. He reluctantly agreed after she mentioned Ellie's name and informed him it would be in his best interest if they met. Josh felt overwhelmed when Sharon filled him in to the fact Ellie had not only infected him with syphilis, but had also made it look like Cindy was involved with more than just sitting with a disturbed hospital patient. She explained the concocted photo. Josh was so distraught with this news he left town and the hospital building project without giving notice and returned to his New York City apartment. A month later, very depressed and drunk out of his mind, he stumbled up the back stairs to the rooftop garden of the tall luxury apartment building where he was living, climbed atop the waist high wall and jumped.

CHAPTER SIXTEEN

Cindy was over overwhelmed with grief upon learning Josh had committed suicide. "If only Josh had let me explain how the picture came to be, this could have been avoided," she brokenheartedly told Jenny McClean as they shared a booth for lunch at the deli. "You need to keep me away from Ellie, or I can't be held responsible for what I might do to her! She is totally responsible for his death!"

Jenny gave a snort while continuing to stir sugar into her iced tea. "You need not worry about seeing Ellie any time soon. I am surprised you don't know, but at the same time, I'm not surprised since you have been living like even more of a hermit since Josh left town and committed suicide. Ellie sneaked out of town without a forwarding address after health department officials ordered tests that revealed she has syphilis. Now that she has left town, they will have to rely on learning who she infected when those individuals turn up at a doctor's office or the clinic for treatment; and everyone thought she was such an angel. Angel, my foot! She is the devils personal handmaiden!"

Jenny stopped talking long enough to take a sip of tea before continuing. "I do not understand why you feel sadness for Josh. Had he kept his pants zipped or listened to you, he would not have ended up sharing her disease or dying! There were people, including Sharon Murphy, who were aware of Ellie's involvement with a lot of men; everyone except you and, apparently, Josh. I don't think he would have been intimate with her when there was a good chance of you becoming his wife, if what I heard from the jewelry store owner is true. Josh was planning to give you an engagement ring and ask you to marry him before seeing that picture."

"Ellie had us all fooled, me included, until it was too late," replied Cindy sadly. Since she rarely paid attention to rumors, she would not learn until later when Sharon Murphy let it slip that Ellie had been paying her with cash and pills to keep quiet by denying rumors regarding Ellie's sexual encounters.

"To give Sharon a tiny bit of credit, she, with reluctance, did reveal the names of men who slept with Ellie to the county health department doctor following Josh's death," offered Cindy. "While a noble gesture, the disclosure makes Sharon just as guilty as Ellie, maybe even more so when she waited to pass along the information. There could be people who unknowingly were infected that Sharon was not aware of, although I doubt it. Perhaps she will take note of just how much of a disaster she created by keeping quiet for so long," declared Cindy between bites of her bacon, lettuce and tomato sandwich.

"Don't hold your breath when it comes to Sharon willingly divulging information," replied Jenny. "I heard the BMW she drives was given to her by Melvin Pendergast, along with monthly payments of five hundred dollars to keep her mouth shut about his alley cat ways. I think his wife Betty was aware, but she liked the deep pockets lifestyle his businesses provided while engaging in her affair with the bartender. I'm sure Sharon was also on the payroll of many other prominent men about town long before Melvin shot himself and Josh committed suicide."

Cindy did not have a ready answer or comment. Instead, she took another bite of her BLT rather than adding to rumors already circulating in reference to this ugly situation. Over the years she learned the hard way that people who present themselves as friends may have another agenda, including well-meaning Jenny.

"Oh dear, I hope I didn't say anything out of line," she mused, watching Jenny walk away after saying their goodbyes in front of the restaurant. Cindy was not surprised to hear via the grapevine that she continues to carry the torch for Josh Morgan the next day. "At least it's good to know my instincts are still intact when it comes to trusting," she said aloud to herself.

CHAPTER SEVENTEEN

Eighteen months passed after Josh leapt to his death from his New York City apartment building. An unexpected knock sounded on Cindy's front door. She was not expecting anyone, having obtained restraining orders to keep news reporters at bay after it became known she and Josh Morgan had a connection. She looked through the door's peep hole. Unfortunately, the person doing the knocking stepped to one side, making it impossible to identify him or her. Unwilling to open the door to an unknown person, she gingerly pushed aside the curtain covering a window located beside the door. She determined the visitor was a man. He turned sideways and started walking toward the porch steps when she recognized David Mercer. She hurried to open the door. "David! Is that you?" she called out joyfully.

"The one and only," he answered with a grin, retracing his steps to stand facing her.

"Please, won't you come in? Sorry I didn't recognize you right away. You stepped out of the peephole line of sight. This forced me to check who was there by pushing the curtain aside on the window beside the door. I know you must think I'm paranoid, but certain events have made me cautious about opening the door. I have found unwelcome reporters on the porch. Several managed to link me to architect, Josh Morgan, the man who jumped off the apartment building in New York City. I'm sure you recall Josh once worked here in Riverwood designing and overseeing building the new hospital wing before he walked away without completing the project," offered Cindy.

David nodded. "Wasn't he the man who came into my hospital room to give you that upsetting picture?" He wanted to add, *and called you a slut*, but he refrained because he knew it would be painful for Cindy to hear that word again in reference to herself.

"Yes, that was him," Cindy replied without adding anything more in reference to Josh. "Would you like to come inside and have some coffee to warm you up? The weather here in early April can be a little chilly."

"Hot coffee would be great," he replied. "I should have called before coming, but I wasn't sure I would be welcome since I didn't try to contact you after I left the hospital," said David.

"Don't be silly," replied Cindy. "It was not your fault Josh made such a scene when he didn't know the facts. You did not owe me anything as to where you had gone following your discharge. Come join me in the kitchen while I make coffee. We have a lot to catch up on since I last saw you. Nobody at the hospital would tell me where you had gone following your discharge. I assumed you were placed in some sort of a . . ."

David held up his hand to stop her from continuing. "I'm sure my behavior left you thinking I was spirited away to a mental hospital, but that didn't happen. When I agreed to see a psychiatrist twice weekly and live in a group home with six other PTSD men in recovery, I never left Riverwood. Since then, I've managed to find peace after learning ways to accept what happened to my buddies and what took place during my capture. I'm proud to say I am now the manager of the home."

"I'm happy to hear the news, but I wish you had tried to contact me," commented Cindy. "I wasn't aware we had such a facility in Riverwood. I'm not aware of a lot, by choice, regarding what goes on in town these days. I spent the winter out here reading, watching TV, knitting sweaters and booties for newborn babies or throws for those in need through contacts at the hospital. I know it is not an exciting life, but those activities help kill time."

"Aren't you still a volunteer at the hospital?" questioned David. "You are certainly well suited for that type of activity."

Cindy hesitated before answering. "I resigned the day after you were discharged," she replied without offering any further explanation.

"What prompted your resignation?" David questioned.

Again, Cindy hesitated before giving an answer. "It's a long story for another time. Tell me about yourself. You look healthy and well rested. You must feel proud to have become manager of the place where you are living," She avoided discussing what happened between Ellie and Josh, her resignation as a volunteer and Josh's suicide, those memories still being very painful.

"The house where I'm living is in a lower middle class, blue collar residential area south of downtown. Those houses were built just prior to World War II ending, when the GI Bill was enacted to enable service men and women to buy affordable housing. Now people living there are elderly. Many don't know their neighbors, or I'm sure there would be an uproar to get rid of what some people consider us undesirable, crazy people. As it stands now, those living close to us think we are great neighbors. We mow lawns for them, run errands or shovel snow for free. People who live on either side or across the street from us often come to barbeques at our house, and we are invited to their parties and cookouts. They think we are just a group of diehard bachelors who haven't found the right girls. One neighbor lady has made it a mission unsuccessfully to pawn me off on her niece as a potential husband."

"I don't mean to be nosy, but are you saying a handsome guy like you doesn't date?" asked Cindy.

David's face turned red, and he squirmed in his chair. "No, I haven't been dating. I wanted to make sure my head was on straight before entering into a relationship with anyone of the opposite sex. I take marriage very seriously. Too bad my ex-wife didn't have the same mindset."

"I am sorry. I didn't realize you were married before," said Cindy.

"Not your fault. I didn't get that far into our talks before being discharged from the hospital."

"Do you want to talk about it now?" asked Cindy.

"That is a story for another time, just like the one involving Josh is for you," said David. "I didn't come all the way out here to talk about the past. I came to find out how you are doing and ask if you would care to go out to dinner with me so we can get to know each other in a less structured environment than a hospital room, like me in restraints raving out of my mind."

Cindy took a deep breath before answering. "Forgive me, but feel I must ask. Are you aware of how ugly rumors can be when people like you and me, both single and living in or near a small town, are seen in public having dinner together?"

"That would be yes, but I'm willing to put up with rumors if it means getting to know you better," answered David. "What you did for me when a lot of others would have written me off as a mental case makes it easy for me to tell the likes of Sharon Murphy and her tribe where to go. I have survived being a Marine, a POW, wife desertion, a thug beating and PTSD. I can survive anything Sharon or her friends dish out. The question in my mind is can you?"

Cindy took several sips of her coffee before answering. "I don't know, but there is only one way to find out. Yes, I will have dinner with you." David did not try to conceal a smile. "How about we have dinner Friday evening at the local diner for starters? You and I might as well begin a friendship by making ourselves known amid the rumor mongers."

"Maybe you might want to give this a little more thought," suggested Cindy. "As it now stands, it would appear Sharon Murphy and members of her small but vicious crowd are unaware of the group home where you live. They all like to think they are the cream of society living up there on the north side in those large, drafty old Victorian houses. Far be it for them to bother with what they consider a lower middleclass neighborhood they feel is beneath them. I imagine they already assigned those living there the dregs of humanity not worth noting. That could change if people like us were to start spending time together in what they view as one of their haunts, such as the diner. Our presence would attract attention. In turn, they might start snooping around to find more about you and your housemates with the reaction a lot of ignorant people have regarding those living in group homes. It would not surprise me if they would start a petition to have you run out of town! I've learned this is how they think. This means we must give serious thought to doing anything which could hurt your roommates or you." *Good heaven! This is the same thing I told Josh*, thought Cindy.

David sat staring across the room giving thought to what Cindy said. "Wow! I never thought about complications like that . . . I guess we do need to give being seen in each other's company a little more thought. It appears my growing up on a farm in Kansas and living on the road for the past five years has left me unaware of how things work in a small town like Riverwood. I never gave a thought to such mentality." He paused to take several sips of coffee. Sensing he had more to say, Cindy remained quiet, allowing him to continue. "My two older brothers didn't want to stay on the farm after mom died, so I bought them out and stayed there. Then I made a big mistake finding a local girl for a wife with the thought of raising a family and living there until we died. But conflict in the Middle East came along. I felt the need to do my part, so I signed up with the Marine Corps. I guess I didn't know how lonely it could get for a woman living out there alone in the middle of nowhere, except for the hired help, along with not knowing for more than two years whether her husband was dead or alive.

"To shorten a long story, after escaping from the POW camp, I spent a short time in a German hospital then was sent home and given an honorable discharge. I tried contacting her from Germany, but she didn't respond. Then I came home to an empty house. The farm manager told me she and one of the hired hands struck up what he described as a very close friendship. This was backed up by friends at the Co-Op. I was already on the edge mentally dealing with what I now know to be PTSD. Learning my wife left me for another man sent me over that edge and led me to take to the road, leaving the running of the farm to the manager my father hired after it became clear he could no longer do manual labor without additional help. Thank God my wife and I did not have children! Now you pretty much know my life's story beyond what we discussed while I was hospitalized."

"I'm the one who should say wow!" remarked Cindy. "It must have been hard for you to come home to find . . . I am at a loss for words to describe what you have endured. I don't mean to get personal, but did you file for divorce, or did she?"

"I filed after not hearing anything from her for three years. I took this step on the advice of an ACLU attorney I met in a bar. But this didn't happen until another year passed. By then I had become a total mental and emotional mess relying on alcohol to make it through the day. I didn't feel the inclination to hire a private investigator to track her down, so rather than having a failed marriage hanging over my head, I took the attorneys advice and filed for divorce on the grounds of desertion. Since I was a veteran, the lawyer went to bat for me, posting required notices in various newspapers asking for her to come forward. When she didn't respond, a district judge granted me a divorce on the grounds of desertion. The rest is history. As far as I know I still own a farm in Kansas. Enough said about me. It's your turn to fill me in about you."

"I thought we weren't going in that direction today," replied Cindy. As a diversion she asked, "Would you like more coffee and a couple of homemade cookies to go with it?" David knew what she was doing but went along with her to a point.

"I would love more coffee and homemade cookies, but not as much as hearing your story. I would feel bad if you didn't trust me after what I just told you." Cindy felt she was being backed into a corner. She got up from her chair and reached for the coffee pot and cookies. David placed his hand on her arm and gave her a pleading look. "Emotional wounds form scabs if not exposed to the light of day. This forms emotional pus increasing until it breaks through creating a mess, or it takes over the life of the one infected like what happened to me. It took a beating at the hands of a gang to start me facing what happened and do something about it."

"Are you sure you weren't a psychiatrist in a former life?" asked Cindy. She returned the coffee pot to the counter after refilling their cups and handed David the plate of cookies.

"No, but life has taught me a lot of things over the past five years. I think the beating at the lake awakened me to the fact I am master of my destiny. You also played a big part in that awakening. Stop stalling, sit down and have a bite of one of these delicious cookies and tell me your story," David insisted.

"But it isn't polite to talk with your mouth full," replied Cindy taking a bite of her cooking, trying to stall a while longer. David shoved half a large cookie in his mouth and began talking.

"See, it can be done. Emily Post or Miss Manners is not here to point out my lack of manners!" The crumbs flying from his mouth caused Cindy to burst out laughing and hand him a fist full of paper napkins.

"You do have a point," she conceded. "Where do I begin . . . I was born in a small clapboard house once standing where this house now stands. I was an only child, age five, when my parents died in an automobile accident. My father's mother, Grammy, and her husband moved out here to raise me, something she never let me forget. My maternal grandparents died before I was born, so I never knew them. I do know we did not have much money. Grammy worked as a waitress at the diner, often leaving me and Gramps, retired, to our own devices. Gramps taught me how to fish, but he died of a heart attack six months after the move here. I was six when that happened. Grammy died when I was barely fifteen. At school I was the butt of jokes because I did not have money to dress like the other kids. The relative who agreed to take over my care after her death had a 'reputation.' Are you sure you want me to continue? My life hasn't been nearly as interesting as yours."

"I think you are about ready to get to the interesting parts," replied David. Perhaps so, thought Cindy, but do I want to relive them? Several more sips of coffee taken, she began again. "I became a ward of the state under the supervision of a distant cousin who was rumored to be the town trollop. Since I was older, and there was a relative willing to care for me, I was not placed in foster care. She took over my care—for the money I might add. There was a steady stream of "uncles" who visited what was my house, according to the court after a will was found. I leave it to your imagination how I was treated by the kids when this cousin moved in with me when I was in high school. The girls wanted nothing to do with me. The boys wanted . . . well you know what the boys wanted!

"I had barely turned nineteen when my cousin died. Full time jobs were not available. I found myself without any means of support beyond a few babysitting and house cleaning jobs. She drained most of what was left of the estate bank account and spent it on herself. I was forced to rely on charity to pay for her burial. That is when I started waitressing at the diner and became the target for . . . for propositions like those directed toward my cousin. I always refused, but that did not stop the rumor mill. It didn't seem to matter that I attended church and Sunday school every week, sang in the church choir and played clarinet in a local group providing music for people in the old folk's home. According to certain people, I was no different than my cousin!" Cindy was struggling.

David knew it yet encouraged her to continue. "Get it out in the open where it can't hurt you anymore," he urged.

Cindy took several more swallows of her cooling coffee before she could continue. "At age twenty-seven, I met a man, Harold Marsh. He was passing through town when he stopped by the diner to have a cup of coffee and piece of pie on his way to Portland. He ended up having four cups of coffee and three pieces of pie, something he later confessed doing to justify lingering at the counter so he could make small talk with me. Not being a local, he was not aware of my alleged reputation. He began making a regular stop at the diner when business in Portland brought him through Riverwood. We ended up dating six months before he asked me to marry him, and I accepted. By the time we were married, he knew rumors were not true concerning my alleged clandestine activities. Unknown to me, Harold turned out to be a very wealthy man. He insisted we demolish the ramshackle house I inherited and build this one." She stopped talking for a moment to gather her composure before continuing. "Harold was a lover of art. That is why I had so many lovely items to sell at the church yard sale. It was a hard decision to sell those things. Seeing them every day was depressing, and I knew it wasn't healthy. . . . I'm sorry. I can't go on. I don't want to make a fool of myself by crying."

"I'm sorry these things happened to you," said David, his voice conveying sincerity. "Now I understand why you stopped going into town, except to buy groceries and gas for your car until you met Josh Morgan. Then you stopped going for the most part again after he left and took his life. In the beginning of what became your relationship with him, I have the feeling Josh stepped into the role Harold had filled. Stop me if I'm wrong."

"You aren't wrong. We got along fine until Ellie Montgomery decided she wanted Josh. For this to happen she had to find with a way to get me out of the picture. She used the fact I am a people pleaser to lure me into becoming a pink lady at the hospital. There she could dictate the hours I was assigned and knew I would not refuse. Now I know she always made sure I was scheduled to volunteer during many of the hours I would have spent with Josh by assigning me to sit with you every evening when you were a patient after the beating. I am sure by now you know how the picture of me laying my head on your bed happened. I was exhausted, and you finally drifted off to sleep around eleven p.m. I had completed my nine-hour assignment as a pink lady volunteer at nine p.m. When I could not keep my eyes open any longer, I laid my head on your bed and dozed off, something I should not have done. This is when Ellie got the idea for the picture—when she checked in to see how things were going. The security guard later confessed Ellie bribed him and threatened the loss of his job, in addition to telling his wife he was cheating, if he didn't sneak into your room and take the picture.

"Ellie set me up! She knew exactly what she was doing when she wouldn't take no for an answer, insisting I become a pink lady! Too bad Josh didn't know her motives and how the picture came about. When he walked in the hospital room that day, probably at the urging of Ellie, to see you giving me an innocent hug, he believed it when she told him we . . . we were more than just patient and sitter. Josh wouldn't listen to me. Instead, he became intimately involved with that piece of trash, only to be infected with a social disease! When it became general knowledge Ellie had syphilis and was having sex with a lot of different men, Josh apparently felt too ashamed to approach me, especially after learning he contracted syphilis by spending time with Ellie. I am reasonably sure this is what made him walk off the job at the hospital, move back to New York City and jump from the roof of his apartment building. It makes me angry and gives me nightmares to think Ellie walked away without paying the price she should have paid! And to think I'm the one Sharon Murphy and her crowd call a slut when Josh and I never had sex!" Cindy felt her throat tighten in anger and tears threaten to spill down her cheeks again.

"I'm sure wherever she is, Ellie is paying the price," said David. "Just so you know, I don't think you are a slut. I think you were, and still are, a true angel of mercy, something I will make sure to inform anyone I meet. I do intend to meet more than a few locals." *Dear God, I hope she doesn't think I'm trying to replace Harold or Josh*, he thought. *I really like this woman and hope we become friends, or even more than friends. First, I need prove myself to be a responsible person who doesn't react negatively when a car backfires, someone yells or something falls to make a loud noise.*

"Thank you," whispered Cindy. "Would you like some cookies to take with you? Your roommates might enjoy them too." She said this as a polite way of letting him know it was time for him to leave. Even though her instincts told her David could be trusted, she didn't want him to linger. Should anyone ask why, she would not have an answer.

David got the message and stood. "Let me go back to my house and talk to the guys about the possibility of us being run out of town if we have dinner at the diner. I think I already know the answer, and I can't wait for you to meet them. They are a great bunch of guys. Is that agreeable with you?"

The tension on Cindy's face lessened. "I would be delighted to meet your roommates. Maybe you can talk them into all of us sitting at the big round table at the deli on Friday," said Cindy. "Call me if you still feel comfortable after talking with them. If they don't think it's a good idea I will understand. In the meantime, take these cookies and be on your way before Sharon Murphy gets wind you are here. She appears to make her business to know my every move these days."

"You let me deal with Sharon Murphy," said David grimly. That said, he put his hands on her shoulders and gave her a quick hug, retrieved his coat from the chair where Cindy had placed it, then hesitated with his hand on the doorknob. "I want you to know I will be out of town for about a week visiting the farm in Kansas starting this coming Monday."

"Why are you making the trip?" asked Cindy. She knew she was being nosey but asked anyway.

David grinned mischievously. "I need to see a man about a horse." This was his way of avoiding an answer when he did not know why, only he needed to go. Cindy followed him out the door to stand on the porch to watch him bound down the stairs and walk toward the car. A sack of cookies in his left hand, keys in his right, she heard him whistling as he walked toward the vehicle borrowed to make the trip to her house.

"I think it's time I checked into selling the farm in Kansas, buying a car, get a few nice clothes, and have a few dollars to court a woman, namely Cindy Marsh," David said to himself. Before he shut the car door he shouted to Cindy as she stood on the porch, "See you at diner on Friday at six. I would offer to come and pick you up, but this is a borrowed car." Cindy let him know she would drive into town and meet him at the diner.

Cindy felt relieved when she met David at the diner to find his buddies also present. They all stood when she was directed to their table by an unsmiling waitress, who happened to be a friend of Sharon Murphy. David reached out his hand to greet her. "Hello Cindy. I would like you to meet my roommates and good friends." He began naming each man and how long they had lived at the residence he now managed. Cindy smiled and greeted each one with a firm handshake and smile, thanking them for coming and for their military service. After being seated, each man studied his menu while sneaking shy looks in her direction before laying his menu aside. The waitress ignored their table for such a long time it prompted David get up from his seat to approach the man he knew to be the owner, Bryan Berry.

"Excuse me, Mr. Berry. My name is David Mercer. I am the former Marine who was beaten by thugs while camping out at the lake. The gentlemen seated at the round table near the back with Cindy Marsh, are also men who served honorably in the military. I assume you are aware the lady, Ms. Marsh, was extremely helpful in my recovery while she was a volunteer at the hospital. We have patiently waited to place an order for more than an hour while observing others who entered after us being served. I was wondering if you could help us order our dinners."

Bryan's face revealed the instant ruddiness of someone who spent a lot of time outdoors—not his usual pasty complexion, but that of embarrassment. "Mr. Mercer," he began. David gave him a disarming smile. "Call me David."

"Please allow me to start again," said Bryan. "First of all, David, let me thank you to you and your friends for your service. I was sorry to hear about the beating. That is not how we like to treat visitors to our community. I heard the sheriff tracked down the culprits. They were arrested for their disgusting actions and sentenced to two years in the county jail." Bryan suddenly experienced a light bulb moment. "Aren't you the guy who saw Melvin Prendergast dump the bodies of Jude in the hospital footer and Grace in Mirror Lake?"

"That would be me," replied David. His immediate reaction was to think Bryan was about to unleash a barrage of derogatory comments because he shed light on the identification of the murderer. But to his surprise that did not happen.

"I need to shake your hand. By you having the courage to step forward, the town has returned to the quaint little village it used to be before everyone feared we had a serial killer in our midst," said Bryan, reaching out his hand for a handshake, and David shook it. "Give me a minute to locate your waitress. You and your friends are having dinner on the house this evening."

"That isn't necessary," said David. "I did not approach you with the idea of getting free meals. We just wanted to order and eat before closing time."

"Oh, but I insist your meals be comped for the inconvenience," replied Bryan with a nervous smile. "I want all of you to return for future meals." Not more than thirty seconds later, loud voices were heard coming from the kitchen, followed by the waitress storming out the diner's front door. While words in the kitchen were muffled, they were able to figure out the waitress said she was not about to wait on that slut, Cindy Marsh, or her male friends. Less than a minute after the waitress made her exit, Bryan appeared, pen and order pad in hand to take their order. "Sorry about that," was all he offered.

"If you need help, I know a fellow who is very good at waiting tables," said David. "He owned a restaurant before finding himself in charge of a mess tent in Afghanistan. David introduced George Slater who said he would be happy to lend a hand. Twenty minutes later everyone was engrossed in eating one of the best meals they had eaten in years. George remained behind to help buss dishes and wait on customers who arrived for a late dinner. Bryan hired him on the spot. After the others said their goodbyes, Cindy asked David to walk with her to her car. "Don't be surprised when good will extended by Barry this evening evaporates," she warned. The waitress who stormed out is one of Sharon Murphy's flunkies. I would be willing to bet money she beat a path straight to Sharon's door the minute she left. And what she had to report was not good, me being the lone female surrounded by seven handsome men."

David frowned. "If that is the case, I need to pay a visit to Ms. Murphy and have a little chat, something I was going to do anyway." He hesitated before asking, "Would it be okay if I came to your house later tomorrow afternoon? I noticed you haven't taken down the storm windows and there will soon be warmer weather. I can take care of that before I leave for Kansas."

"I would love to have you visit, but there is no need for you to remove storm windows. We will have nicer weather in about three weeks. This is something I can do. I should have done it last week, but after everything happened with Ellie, then learning Josh committed suicide I . . . didn't get around to doing it," replied Cindy. David's heart ached for what Cindy was experiencing through no fault of her own. He wanted to take her in his arms and tell her everything would be alright but knew it would take time before that happened, less time if what he planned to do would make a significant difference. "I'll be there around three tomorrow. I would be there sooner, but I have important business to take care of first." Originally sad at leaving the restaurant and Cindy, David felt a surge of happiness knowing he would be spending more time with her tomorrow.

Cindy was unaware David and Sharon Murphy were cousins or he had visited her in Riverwood as a child; something he remembered during a session with his psychiatrist but kept to himself after receiving a packet of information from the farm's manager prior to his scheduled visit. The package arrived overnight by UPS when the manager learned David was coming for a visit. The package, in addition to reports, contained a note David recognized as shaky handwriting of the elderly farm manager. It stated vaguely that David would be interested in additional information awaiting him upon arrival in Kansas. David shook his head. "Too bad he didn't let me know in the note what *kind* of information so I could be prepared. I sure hope it isn't concerning my ex showing up on the doorstep wanting me to take her back! That is not going to happen!"

David stood on the sidewalk and looked up the hill toward the pale-yellow Victorian house with dark green trim where Sharon Murphy was living. He took a deep breath before walking up nine, wide, sweeping steps onto the large front porch to ring the doorbell. His felt apprehensive because they had not been in contact since David was a child. He was unsure she would recognize him. He noticed white lace curtains covering tall, leaded glass windows beside the door being pushed aside by a sour-faced woman who let them drop before she answered the door. Opening the door about three inches, she spoke, "Who are you and what do you want?" she demanded.

Even though he suspected she knew who he was, David decided to play along. "My name is David Mercer. If you are the Sharon Murphy who once lived in Kansas before relocating in Riverwood, we are cousins. I would like to have a chat with you."

"Is that so?" questioned Sharon without opening the door wider. "If you are here for a handout, you're out of luck!"

David stood his ground, sticking the toe of his shoe between the door and door jamb to prevent her from closing it. "I am not here for a handout. I am here to have a chat with you. Nothing more, nothing less. You may have heard about me. I am the man who was beaten when camping at the lake and ended up a patient at the local hospital."

"I'm aware of what happened. What does that have to do with me?" snapped Sharon.

"I will be happy to fill you in on the details if you will grant me the opportunity," said David. "If you need proof of who I am, my mother's brother, Silas, married your mother, Marie. They lived in Kansas."

Sharon tilted her head and gave him a sideward glance as though in thought. "Anybody can look up marriage records. Where did they live? Did they live in town or on a farm? How many children did they have and what are their names?" she questioned in rapid fire. David answered her questions without hesitation. Only then did she open the door wider and motion for him to enter and take a seat on the elegant brocade settee in the parlor. Sharon perched stiffly on a Queen Anne chair across from him, legs crossed primly at the ankles, hands folded in her lap. The look on her face was one as though she smelled something unpleasant as she studied David's face. "Now I see some family traits in your face and build," she admitted. "But the question remains. Why are you here, and what do you want? We have not seen each other in twenty-five years. As I recall, I was not invited to your wedding, not that I would have attended. The woman you were marrying was known to be lacking in character. She did not belong in our family! But I suppose love is blind and you are still married to her?"

"With your ability to snoop on the lives of people around here, I'm surprised you aren't aware she walked off and left me when I was a POW in Afghanistan while serving in the marines," remarked David.

"Ah, yes. I did hear something about that now that you mention it," remarked Sharon.

"You are very good a just happening to hear things about people, aren't you?" questioned David. He did not miss she bristled at his comment. This did not stop him from proceeding. "That is the reason I am here. I heard rumors initiated by you concerning Cindy Marsh. I am here to tell you, not ask you, to stop this nonsense immediately! Cindy is a lovely, innocent and trustworthy person. You have systematically gone out of your way with efforts to make people believe she should be wearing a scarlet letter on her forehead! I want it to stop! Do I make myself clear?"

Sharon immediately jumped to her feet, a look of indignation on her face. "How dare you come into my home and accuse me of trying to sully the reputation of that woman, a woman I have reason to believe sleeps around indiscriminately! You need to get out of my house this very minute!"

David did not get up. "Sharon, I hate to be the one to break the news, but you do not own this house. I do. You moved here from a boarding house following your marriage to William Murphy. This house and contents were left to me after my mother and father died. I allowed the two of you to live here rent free, you apparently believing your husband owned it, even after he died. He only rented it from my parents and stopped paying rent after my mother passed away nine years ago. Why Dad didn't follow up on collecting rent, I do not know. Due to the process of settling his estate after his death, and a promise made to my dear mother on her death bed, I did not pursue collecting rents and allowed you to continue living here following William's death."

"What do you mean this is not my house? We had no children. William's estate was left to me," she replied fervently.

"Did you see a will prepared by an attorney or William?" asked David.

Sharon admitted she had not seen a deed to the house or a will, nor did William's estate go through probate. This was not unusual at that time of his death when Riverwood was an outpost suitable only for a vacation destination where men of wealth indulged in fishing at Mirror Lake while maintaining family estates in Seattle or Portland.

"But . . . but nobody ever questioned me continuing to live here after my husband died, and I have continued to receive a monthly deposit into my checking account large enough to keep food on the table and minimal clothing on my back," sputtered Sharon. This statement belied opulent surroundings and manner of her fashionable dress which did not go unnoticed by David. "You never thought to find out where this money comes from?" he questioned.

"No. The money is deposited directly into my checking account. I was under the impression it came from my late husband's estate."

"Just so you know, William died penniless. I paid for his funeral and debts. I am the one who set up monthly payments into your checking account and allowed you to live here rent free at the request of my mother. I'm surprised with your ability to gather information; you claim to be unaware she and my father bought this house for a getaway retreat without you knowing William did not own it."

"How would I know he didn't own this house? Back then women were not expected to know such things. A husband was expected to take care of such matters. I had no reason to think the house and contents were not left to me after William died. In fact, do you have proof you own this house?" David reach into his jacket pocket and produced the title and copy of the will. Sharon looked at the documents, then forcefully handed them to him. He calmly folded and returned them to his jacket pocket. "You didn't think I would come here without proof of ownership, did you?" Sharon merely sniffed, sat down and did not answer.

"Mom asked me to plan for you to continue living here, even though you were not kind to her when you attempted to make everyone in our family believe she was unfaithful to my father. Just so you know, she was faithful to him, and he knew it. That is why he stayed married to her while you became an outcast as far as our family and friends were concerned; enough of an outcast you moved. I am here today to inform you if you persist in causing Cindy Mercer any further harm to her reputation, you will find yourself out on the street, and everyone in this town will know why. Your husband and you were living here on charity, as you continue to do. Now do I make myself clear?"

Sharon leaned back farther into the chair and covered her face with her hands. "I had no idea you, of all people, owned this house and your mother made it possible for me to live here." Then she removed her hands, straightened her shoulders, and stood ramrod straight. "Of course, I will have an attorney investigate this matter. It is time for you to leave!"

"If you choose to initiate legal action, be ready for a counter suit to collect rents due and unpaid for as many years as the law allows, along with being prepared to find a way to pay your living expenses and find living quarters elsewhere. This is in addition to everyone becoming aware of money you charge certain individuals to keep their reputations intact." Sharon gave him a startled look. David smiled. "Does it surprise you I am aware of how you extort certain people in this town? Snooping must be a family trait. How do you think I learned about you? Think about it. You have a lovely old home in which to live and money in the bank to more than meet your needs. Are you ready to give this up, along with your questionable social status in Riverwood? It is not like I am asking anything more of you and your small circle of friends than to stop making life miserable for people when none of you have solid evidence of their misbehavior. You use only speculation to what you consider their immoral ways to hurt them. You are not God. Even if you happen to have unsavory information about people, which I am sure you do, it is not your right to judge others or broadcast it to the world! That is why we have a court system, should those wronged choose to make use of it. Do I have your word that rumors will stop, along with taking money to keep quiet, not only concerning Cindy Marsh, but everyone else in this town as of right this minute?"

Sharon found herself sitting down again. Her sense of indignation and self-importance deflated like an overinflated balloon hit dead center by a dart. She looked up at her cousin, eyes pleading for mercy. "I promise," she replied meekly.

"Sharon, I am sorry it has become necessary for us to become reacquainted under these circumstances, but you leave me no choice. I would like to acknowledge you publicly as a family member, but not while you continue living this way. I am in the process of learning it is never too late to start over. I strongly suggest you do the same. You might be amazed how forgiving people can be in a small town if given a good reason to forgive. You could start by letting everyone know you were mistaken about Cindy having affairs with men. In fact, I strongly suggest as a humble pie response, you bake and deliver a pie to her, along with an apology for false rumors you have attributed to her as fact. Think of it as confession is good for the soul." Sharon continued to sit staring at him while thinking he was out of his mind. "Thank you for your time. Please do not bother to get up. I can see myself out. Just keep in mind I will follow through to make sure you have at the very least attempted to take the right path," said David.

It took fewer than five minutes after David left before Sharon came to her senses. "Like hell I will bake a pie and apologize to that woman! If he thinks he can force me into leaving this house or continuing my quest to keep certain individuals on the hook, he is sadly mistaken! This has been my home for the past forty years, and it will continue to be my mission to keep certain people in line! I do not care about the lack of a will or deed! I will see David Mercer dead first!" She reached for the telephone sitting on the table beside her chair and dialed.

"Hello Rex, Sharon Murphy here. I need you to do a favor . . . Stop whining! I haven't told you what it is . . . Yes, I know my request for favors can be inconvenient . . . but not nearly as inconvenient as your wife and the sheriff learning about that cabin in the woods where you entertain a variety of underage girls . . . Do not dare raise your voice to me! I will not tolerate it! . . . That's better. Apology accepted. Now be quiet and listen! I need you to set fire to a certain house located in the lower middleclass section of town close to that so-called night club once owned by Melvin Prendergast . . . That's right. The house where former Marine David Mercer is living along with six of his ex-military buddies . . . Spare me! I want it done at two a.m. on Monday morning when everyone is asleep, including members of the volunteer fire department . . . Shut up and listen! Make sure it goes up like a tinder box with no survivors . . . You heard me correctly, no survivors . . . Do not tell me you are suddenly squeamish when it comes to setting a fire! You will do as you are told, or else I will make sure you face charges for molesting children, and you know what happens in prison to child molesters!"

Sharon slammed down the receiver to sit in twisted contemplation for her next move. "On second thought, I *will* bake a pie for Cindy Marsh. She is the cause of all my problems just by having been born. I would have been the wife of her father had he not gotten her mother pregnant and had to marry her instead of me. After being humiliated when he practically left me standing at the altar, I ended up with what turned out to be a poor excuse of a husband, William Murphy. That lying bastard led me to believe he owned this house and had money in the bank, so I do not feel one bit bad about his mysterious death. He, too, liked my homemade pie so much so it killed him, and nobody ever questioned his death. Such a lucky break for me. How convenient everyone knew he was overweight and had a serious heart problem; and old Doc Stevens told the county coroner an autopsy was not necessary. Yes indeed, another pie will take care of one more problem."

Reinforced by knowledge she had gotten away with murder regarding her husband's death, Sharon believed she could get away with murder again. She arrived early Monday morning at the fire scene to watch flames destroy the man who wanted to take away her house and expose her misdeeds should she not capitulate to his wishes. She was giddy. "Nobody has the right to tell me where I can live or how I should act," she said to her pet cat who accompanied her to the group home for the car ride. "I have overseen calling the shots in this town for a long time and will continue to call them when I think they need to be called. Besides, how can I continue living in the lap of luxury without payments from wrongdoers to keep my mouth shut on behalf of some of our most outstanding citizens?

"As for Cindy Marsh, she does not deserve to live! She is nothing but a tramp pretending to do good works. Any single woman in her right mind would not agree to spend time with that drifter after fawning over him in the hospital, let alone allow him to spend nights in her home! The women of this town should be grateful to me for closing in on those who cheat on their spouses or lead immoral lives! What I am doing is not a crime! As for the pie, Cindy will have eaten the evidence and we will be rid of one more slut! As a bonus, I will not have to look at her and remember her father practically left me standing at the altar! With David Mercer and his unsavory friends out of the way, I will continue to keep certain people in line and live the life I deserve, not one living in poverty due to the lies of that son-of-a bitch I ended up marrying!"

A visitor strolling near the house that afternoon might see kitchen window wide open, smell baking pie, and hear Sharon singing a hymn at the top of her lungs and think that a happy, well-adjusted woman lived there. Nothing would have been further from the truth!

CHAPTER EIGHTEEN

David found Cindy sitting in a chair at the glass topped patio table on her front deck enjoying a glass of iced tea on a temperate late April day. Her home was the first place he headed upon return from his trip to check on the farm in Kansas. He could hardly wait to let her know he decided against selling the farm after finding it in good shape, money in the bank left by his father and a report of projected good crops according to the manager. During David's absence, the now elderly man made sure other hands kept fields and grounds, including rose gardens, barns, outbuildings and the house in pristine condition, just as David's father insisted be continued after his death. Calvin Mercer never gave up hope his son was alive and would return. He had gone so far as to set aside money in a secret account for the farm's upkeep. He failed to mention this to anyone except the manager who was not to reveal the account existed, especially to David's wife, until his son returned and began living on the farm. He kept it to himself he never fully trusted David's wife.

"Hello stranger," remarked a delighted Cindy. She ran to meet him coming up the walkway with open arms. "I'm happy to see you made it back safely. How were things back in Kansas after having been gone for the past five years?"

Following a lingering hug and chaste kiss on the cheek David took a seat opposite her at the table.

"A whole lot better than expected," he replied. "Everything looked pretty much like I left it before I made the mistake of taking off. I could kick myself for having left, but had I stayed, there is no doubt I would have become a worthless alcoholic. I wouldn't have met you or come to terms with what happened when I was a Marine or POW."

"But you might have met someone special, married her and had a family after you divorced your wife if you had stayed," said Cindy.

David shook his head. "I wasn't in any shape for that to happen. If I had stayed, there is no doubt I would have been committed to a mental institution or dead. I have you to thank for that not happening." He hesitated before continuing. "In case you haven't figured it out, I'm in love with you, not just grateful for the part you played in my recovery. That is why didn't stay in Kansas. I came back here to find out if you have feelings for me beyond that of a caretaker and friend." David held his breath waiting for her response.

"I . . . I don't know what to say. I do like you a lot, David, but we have not spent enough alone time together to know each other. Most of our time has been spent in the company of your friends and the ladies they brought to my house for a few meals. I would like to get to know you on a one-to-one basis. What I am trying to say is, I do have feelings for you, but let's not rush into a relationship we could later regret," replied Cindy.

David gave her what amounted to a forced smile. "That is all I needed to know. I didn't expect you to fall into my arms without being properly courted."

"But courting me openly could be a problem when it comes to Sharon Murphy and her need to spread rumors," replied Cindy. "In case you haven't noticed, the woman hates me. Why, I do not know, beyond me avoiding her whenever possible."

"Trust me, Sharon will no longer be a problem, nor will any of her friends. She and I had a little talk before I left for Kansas."

"Now that you mention it, Sharon did come by to pay a visit and brought a homemade elderberry pie. She apologized for rumors she spread about me. I didn't have the heart to tell her I'm allergic to elderberries. After she left, I tossed the pie on the compost heap. A few days later I noticed a lot of dead field mice out there, along with a red fox. I am left to assume they must have died after nibbling at it. I saw this when I went out to deposit eggshells and coffee grounds left from breakfast."

This information sent a chill up David's spine. "Is there any of the pie left?" he asked.

"I assume so since about half of it was still there when I went out there after breakfast," replied Cindy. "Why are you asking?"

Ignoring her question, David asked, "Do you have plastic bags and some gloves? I would like to have a sample of that pie analyzed."

"Whatever for?" questioned Cindy. "Sharon was merely trying to say she was sorry for the way she treated me in the past."

David again ignored her question. "Make it three plastic bags—one for a pie sample, one for remains of several dead mice and a larger one for the dead fox. Then we need to burn the remainder of the pie and any dead animals, then bury the ashes deep and place rocks on top of them so other animals can't dig them up."

"David, you are scaring me! What are you trying to say?"

David stopped pacing to face her. "From what you just told me concerning dead mice and fox makes me think there was poison in the pie. Thank God you are allergic to elderberries!"

Cindy stood with a look of confusion. "Why would Sharon want to poison me? I have never done anything except ignore her whenever possible. I have not verbally or physically attacked her when she has gone out of her way to spread rumors about me anyone who really knows me would not believe."

"I didn't want to tell you, but I have done a little snooping to learn there was a time when Sharon and your father were lovers until your mother caught his attention. Your mother ended up pregnant with you and they were married. Sharon was devastated after telling everyone your father was going to marry her, although there is no evidence he proposed. According to old timers I spoke with, he never offered an engagement ring or proposed. It would appear in her twisted mind that you are the cause of why she ended up in an unhappy marriage with another man just to save face after telling friends she was going to marry your father."

Cindy slumped down in her chair. "Oh my God! All these years Sharon has blamed me as the cause for my father not marrying her! How sick is that?"

"Very sick. Apparently sick enough she wanted you dead," replied David. "Until I get lab test results back on these samples, you are not to eat anything Sharon offers, nor should you be alone with her. If she comes here to your house again, don't answer the door and call me."

"But . . . "

"No buts! This woman could prove to be dangerous! Promise me you will not have any contact with her until the pie and dead animals are proven clean of poison," insisted David.

Cindy closed her eyes and shook her head. "We should be celebrating your return from Kansas, and here we sit talking about Sharon Murphy and her sick mind, along with possible poison in a pie! I vote we go inside and make pizza. I am starving! And, before you mention it again, I promise not to have any contact with Sharon until you give me the green light. If there turns out to be poison in her pie, you can be sure I intend to have more than just a few words with Sharon!"

"Pizza sounds good to me," replied David. "I like onions, artichokes, cheese and pepperoni. What do you like?"

That man can read my mind, thought Cindy. "One pizza with the mentioned items coming right up," she announced.

CHAPTER NINETEEN

He laid down his pen and shoved the report aside to answer the phone, though annoyed by the intrusion. "Sheriff Heinz speaking. How can I help you?" The muffled voice on the other end of the line immediately put him on guard; *this could be a prank caller.*

"I know something you should know," the voice began.

"Alright. I'm listening. Spit it out and be quick about it!" declared the sheriff.

The voice continued. "I know this is going to sound crazy, but I have it on good authority the house where David Mercer and his buddies live is going to be torched on Sunday night, make that early Monday morning at two a.m. I know who ordered it done."

"You are right. It does sound crazy," replied the sheriff dourly. "If this is a prank call, it isn't funny."

"I can assure you this is NOT a crank call! I'm the one Sharon Murphy called to do the torch job."

"Is that so? Why should I believe you? I know Sharon can be a more than a little wacko but ordering the burning of a house with sleeping occupants is not her style. She is known for rumors, not murder."

"I'm telling you she ordered me to burn the place down or she was going to start the rumor that I . . . I engage in sexual activities with minors."

"Do you?" asked the sheriff. There was a long pause. When the caller didn't answer, the sheriff asked, "What do you want me to do? Stand guard at this house all night?"

"If that's what it takes to prevent seven ex-military men from being killed," replied the voice. "We both know those cheap cracker box houses will go up like gasoline tossed on a pile of bone-dry brush."

"This conversation would make a whole lot more sense if you would give me your name. Then we could both stand watch," replied the sheriff, trying to keep the caller on the line long enough to trace the call. "I'm listening, but this whole thing would be more believable if you give me your name," repeated the sheriff.

"That isn't happening. You have been warned. Now it is up to you to prevent it from happening, but just in case you decide to sit on your thumbs and waste time trying to trace this call instead of acting, I am going to warn David Mercer."

Sheriff Heinz found himself holding the receiver after the line went dead. "Damn prank caller! Damn outdated call tracing equipment! Sharon would never resort to having that house set on fire! The caller is just some idiot I arrested trying to blow smoke up my ass for retaliation!" That said he slammed down the receiver and went back to finishing his monthly reports.

David Mercer's cell phone began to ring just as he was entering his bedroom at the half-way house. He allowed it to continue ringing until he closed and locked the door behind him. "Hello," was all he said.

"Am I speaking to David Mercer?" asked the caller.

"This is David. Who are you?"

"My name isn't important. The information I need to tell you is important, so listen carefully. I will not repeat it. Sharon Murphy asked me to set fire to the house where you and your six friends are currently living. I will happen early Monday morning, at two a.m. to be precise."

The male caller hung up before David could ask questions. He stared at the cell phone clutched in his hand. "So, Sharon plans to play hard ball," he mused in an almost inaudible voice. "She is sicker than I thought. I wonder if she asked someone to make the call just to scare me, or was that guy serious?" The words of a former squad commander echoed in his mind; "Expect the best, but always prepare for the worst."

David thought aloud, "I need to come up with a plan in case what I've been told could actually happen," he murmured. Only then did the hair on his arms stand on end at the thought Sharon could be responsible for causing something this terrible. "Time for a meeting of the troops," he said aloud as he unlocked and opened his bedroom door to begin shouting at the top of his voice, "Front and center on the double!" Six grumbling men in various states of dress arrived in the hallway to assemble in front of David's door. "At ease," said David out of habit.

"What the hell is this all about?" asked one of the men. "It's Sunday evening. We are all here and none of us are drunk or drugged out.

"And no, there aren't any women in the house," stated another voice.

"Yeah, what gives?" groused another man. "You know we've all been towing the line."

"All of you need to keep quiet and listen. What I have to say is serious," admonished David. The group fell silent and listened to what he had to say before voicing disbelief.

"You're standing here telling us that crazy old broad, Sharon Murphy, wants to fry all of us just because you asked her to stop spreading rumors?" asked John.

"There is more to it," said David. "I own the house where Sharon lives. I told her to stop spreading rumors or I would toss her out on the street. She was under the false impression she owned the house after the death of her husband. It seems the slimy bastard told her and everyone else he owned it when he only rented it from my parents. I have been allowing her to live there as a promise made to my mother on her death bed. I hate to admit it, but Sharon is a cousin. I also have good reason to believe she tried to poison Cindy Marsh." The information regarding Cindy got their attention even more so when David related the story of how Sharon felt she was practically left standing at the altar by Cindy's father. "This belief caused Sharon to take her anger out on Cindy for him marrying her mother and for Cindy having been born. You don't have to tell me this is a sick way to deal with what happened, but the woman hates Cindy as much if not more than her deceased husband."

"What do you want us to do about it?" questioned two of the men simultaneously.

"I strongly suggest we all get dressed in battle fatigues and become a welcoming committee for anyone who attempts to set fire to this house," said David. "Unless you think I should call the sheriff and let him know about the phone call and let him and his deputies handle it."

"What can those deputies and that old geezer do except yell, 'Halt in the name of the law?'" asked Al.

"I say we take matters into our own hands. Then we contact the sheriff when we have the culprit or culprits by the scruff of the neck!" chimed in Jake. Everyone agreed.

By one-thirty a.m. on Monday morning, all seven of them, dressed in fatigues, were in position outside where they could not be seen but had full view of the house. At five minutes until two, Sharon's BMW, its lights off, approached and parked half a block away. At precisely two a.m., a figure dressed in black began to pour liquid Sharon thought was gasoline around the foundation. Only it wasn't gasoline, it was water in a gasoline can. Then smoke began to billow from behind the house. This is when Sharon, thinking the house was on fire, exited her car for a closer look at what she thought would be the demise of David and his friends. This is when she found herself surrounded by seven men wearing combat fatigues. The man dressed in black who gave the impression he poured gasoline around the foundation disappeared into the darkness.

"Hello Sharon," said David. "Did you come prepared to roast marshmallows and hotdogs? Sorry to disappoint you. Hello, sheriff. Looks like you arrived just in time to prevent a mass murder and read Sharon her rights before you haul her off to jail." Then he turned to face Sharon again. "Just so you know, Sharon, I've arranged for samples of the pie you took to Cindy Marsh to be checked for poison. Has this been worth it? I would have allowed you to live in my house and would have paid your bills until your death. All you had to do was stop spreading rumors."

Sharon put on the performance of someone wronged by sinking to the ground in a fit of tears. "I had nothing to do with any of this! Sheriff, you must believe me! I was simply out for a drive when I spotted smoke coming from . . . wait a minute . . . what happened to the smoke? The house should be fully engulfed in flames by now with all that gasoline poured around the foundation!"

"One of the volunteer firemen on standby poured water from a garden hose in an old fifty-gallon drum filled with dead leaves, then he tossed a match into it at two a.m.," said the sheriff. He failed to mention the anonymous caller called him again to suggest faking gasoline in exchange for water and setting fire to a drum filled with dried leaves. "I arranged for the volunteer fire department to make a quiet appearance a block over from the targeted house just in case the caller decided to use gasoline. Sharon Murphy, you are under arrest for soliciting murder by arson. You have the right to remain silent. Anything you say can be used against you in a court of law. If you cannot afford an attorney, one will be appointed for you. Do you understand what I've just said?" Sharon merely nodded. "I also reserve the right to file additional charges of attempted murder if lab reports show poison in the pie you took to Ms. Marsh."

Sharon stared at him with a look of disbelief. "Aren't you going to arrest Rex Slater? He's the one who was to have started the fire!" she demanded indignantly, totally ignoring the pie remark.

"Didn't you hear what I just told you when I read you your rights? Do you realize you are incriminating yourself by trying to implicate Rex?" asked the sheriff.

"I don't give a damn! If I'm going down, so is he!" declared Sharon.

"None of us saw Rex anywhere in the area, so why are we supposed to believe you?" asked David. "All any of us saw was a figure dressed in black who disappeared while we were taking up our positions. We have no idea who it was, something we are willing to testify to in a court of law."

Sharon began flinging her arms and screaming obscenities as the sheriff and David struggled to place her in handcuffs before unceremoniously depositing her into the back seat of the unmarked cruiser. "All you bastards deserve to die!" she shouted. "God appointed me to make sure that will happen! All of you friggin' crazy, immoral bastards, including you, Sheriff Heinz!" Sharon's shouts diminished appreciably when the sheriff closed the patrol car door and stepped back to address David and his friends. "Nice work, boys. If any of you are former MP's and want to become deputies, see me in the morning. I could sure use extra hands come summer when tourists will be flocking to the lake once word gets out Riverwood will be gaining an up and coming, first-class tourist attraction."

"What do you mean making a statement like that?" asked David. "Riverwood will continue to be a sleepy little mountain town with a few specialty stores, a couple of restaurants, bars and a spring fed-lake with edible fish."

The sheriff gave him a knowing grin. "No, I don't think it will stay a sleepy little town. It has just been confirmed, Melvin Prendergast left almost all his fortune to Cindy Marsh with the understanding she will arrange for development of a five-star resort, including a golf course, spa and restaurant on the north end of Mirror Lake where he owned one hundred acres just a stone's throw from his condos. That will bring the wealthy here from up and down the coast to check it out. The only stipulation is she name the restaurant Gracie's." There were more stipulations, but the sheriff decided not to go into them at this time without Cindy and her attorney present.

"What?" said David in utter disbelief. "Cindy hasn't mentioned any of this to me. I thought Melvin's estate was settled months ago."

"Cindy doesn't know any of this, yet. I strongly suggest all of you keep it under your hat for the time being," replied the sheriff. "The clerk of courts was just given what appears to be Melvin's final will late yesterday afternoon. The cleaning crew working in Melvin's office found it while clearing out his desk the same afternoon. At first, they thought it was just scrap paper until Jeanie, the head cleaning woman, brought it to me saying she thought it might be important. We all know she can't read, so she thought I needed to take a look. I checked with the attorney named on the document. He tells me its legit. I'll be letting Cindy know in the morning," said the sheriff.

"But Melvin has been dead for eighteen months. Why did Jeanie wait so long before cleaning, or to bring the will to your attention?" questioned David.

"Melvin's ex-wife Betty filed an injunction preventing anyone from entering or touching anything in the real estate office until the estate went through probate and she ended up with a large chunk of change. The case was settled early Friday morning, allowing the cleaning crew to enter. That is when Jeanie found the will shoved to the back in one of Melvin's desk drawers ... when she and her crew were given the okay to start cleaning. You need not feel bad for Betty. She ended up getting a lot of money out of the deal before anyone knew about the latest will. In fact, Cindy could file suit against Betty and recoup the award she received, but I can't see her doing such a thing. She has too much class, and I'm sure she knows, via the rumor mill, what Betty endured while married to Melvin." Then he bid them all a good night, or what was left of it, got in the cruiser and drove away with

Sharon thrashing around in the back seat and to loudly proclaim her innocence.

"Gentleman, I think it's time we go inside and meet in my room for some coffee and homemade cookies, thanks to Cindy for the cookies. And thank goodness only a couple of our elderly neighbors woke up during all this chaos, and we are all alive!" said David. It took fewer than five minutes after returning inside the halfway house for all the cookies to disappear. The men slapped each other's backs for what turned out to be a good thing their lives were spared, in addition to the culprit ordering their demise caught and hauled off to jail, preventing what could have been life threatening if Sharon's plan had been carried out.

"Do you believe what that crazy woman tried to do?" asked Sam, one of David's roommates. "If that guy she contacted hadn't chickened out and called you and the sheriff, we would all be dead!"

"Well, we aren't dead, so I strongly suggest we get some much-needed sleep," said David with a yawn. "This has been one hell of a crazy night!"

CHAPTER TWENTY

Cindy was on her way to the house after taking inedible breakfast scraps to the compost pile near the side garden. She happened to look around the corner of the house to catch a glimpse of the sheriff's patrol car approaching on the county road. Her stomach tightened when it slowed and pulled into her driveway. *I wonder what he wants now*, she could not help thinking. She quickly walked across the side yard and mounted the steps onto the front porch to keep him from entering the house unless he had a warrant.

"Good morning, Cindy," offered Sheriff Heinz with a friendly smile on his face and a thick manila envelope in his right hand.

"Morning," she mumbled in return. She did not miss the fact he used her given name instead of referring to her as Ms. Marsh as he had done on previous encounters. "What brings you out here Sheriff? Have I done something against the moral code of this town according to Sharon Murphy? Am I to presume a law was passed preventing me from dating David Mercer?" Eyes focused on the manila envelope in his hand, she added, "Don't tell me you have more incriminating pictures!"

"Now don't get all huffy! I've come to give you what could be good news. That's if you will allow me to come inside where we can go over these papers, and no, there are not any more pictures, nor are there any questions pertaining to Grace or Jude's death. Both cases were closed after I figured out David was telling the truth about what he witnessed, along with the note Melvin Pendergast left admitting responsibility to both deaths before he shot himself."

"Well in that case, you may come inside as long as you don't intend to give me the third degree again," offered Cindy.

"Our conversation will not include any questioning, but you may want to be seated when you learn what I've come to tell you."

"I don't think that will be necessary. Whatever you have to say couldn't possibly be more earth shattering than what I've already experienced, so come inside, but I prefer to remain standing."

The sheriff wrinkled his forehead and shrugged his shoulders. "Okay, but don't say I didn't warn you. I am here to deliver a copy of Melvin Prendergast's last will and testament. He named you to receive the bulk of his one $156.5-billion-dollar estate. It is to be used to create a five-star lodge with tennis courts, spa, Olympic-size pool, bath house, golf course and restaurant situated on one hundred acres he owned on the north end of Mirror Lake. This is in addition to compensation for you. The only major stipulation I noted is that you must name the restaurant Gracie's. This amount is in addition to four million he left to his wife Betty and several hundred thousand and some personal effects to a cousin, both of whom have both already received those bequests."

Cindy gasped and took on the appearance of having seen a ghost. "If this is your idea of a joke, it's a bad one."

"Take a look at the will, then tell me if you think I'm joking." He handed the document to her. "You look like you need to sit, or you will fall down," he commented dryly.

Cindy disregarded his instructions to sit, continuing to stand while she skimmed through the document. "Are you sure this is legitimate? I knew Melvin had a lot of money, but $156.5 billion in addition to his businesses and other bequests? This is insane! I didn't even know the man well. Why would he leave such a huge amount of money to me to carry out this plan? This does not make sense!"

"Who knows why he did what he did, but I'm sure the will is legitimate. I spoke to the attorney who drew it up, along with both people who witnessed Melvin's signature. They are willing to testify Melvin had full control of his faculties when he signed the new will."

"But why would leave me the bulk of his estate when we weren't even friends?" sputtered Cindy as she slumped into a nearby chair in a state of total disbelief.

"He left a sealed letter with the attorney to be opened on the date that turned out to be the day he committed suicide, saying how sorry he was Sharon Murphy made your life miserable all those years, when they both knew you didn't deserve it and he didn't speak up," stated the sheriff. "Speaking of Sharon Murphy, I arrested her last night on suspicion of ordering the house burned down where David Mercer and his buddies live. Charges will also be filed if positive lab results show arsenic in the samples of dead animals who ate the pie she gave you."

"I am aware of the attempt to burn the house. David called to let me know," was all Cindy could say as the will fluttered to the floor. She gripped the arms of the chair when the reality of all the sheriff said hit her squarely in the face. "That pie Sharon brought me could have resulted in my death. Oh, my god! And the houses where David and his friends live are all built of wood construction and more than eighty years old. They had no chance had there been a fire!" The sheriff reassured her the attempt was thwarted without going into detail. Cindy continued to sit trying to decide if she was having a bad dream. "Why in the world would Sharon do something so drastic? She had to know if I ate the pie, it would have resulted in my death, and the deaths of everyone living in the halfway house had it burned? Why did she take such drastic measures?"

"According to David, he went to have a talk with Sharon, who turns out to be his cousin, regarding her spreading of rumors. He informed her he owned the house in which she is living, and if she didn't "change her ways" he would take her to court, charge back rent and have her evicted. Apparently to stop that from happening, she decided to have him killed rather than submit to his demand. Thank goodness the person she contacted to do the job chickened out. He called David and me. There is more to the story, but you need to hear it from David."

Confusion deepened on Cindy's face. The deadpan expression Sheriff Heinz was famous for exhibiting became replaced with empathy when she asked, "Doesn't Sharon own the house where she has lived for more years than I've been alive? I thought she inherited it from her husband after he died."

"A lot of other people thought so too. Years ago, nobody bothered to check ownership status, or if there was a handwritten will or one drawn up by an attorney. It was assumed the male head of the household bequeathed his worldly goods to his next of kin, in this case Sharon, since there were no children involved. Her what turned out to be less than truthful husband, told everyone he owned the house outright. Nobody questioned it forty years ago. You must remember that back then Riverwood was only a group of about fifteen Victorian houses built by the very rich from Portland and Seattle and used as summer homes. Those monstrosities were built before soldiers with families began coming home from the second World War with little money, making it necessary for cheaper houses to be built on land their parents or relatives owned. I know it is hard for you to imagine, but there wasn't a courthouse or police department here until only ten years before you were born," offered the sheriff.

"This is all so overwhelming," said Cindy. "What happens if I decide not to proceed with a resort?"

"Who knows? There could be an out, or you could end up being a multi-billionaire. Just be ready for relatives you didn't know existed to come out of the woodwork, along with a lot of people with sob stories who want a cut. A violent chill shook Cindy's body when what he said began to fully sink in. "That means Sharon intended to kill me, too, doesn't it?" she whispered.

"I'm afraid so," he responded. "Thank God you are allergic to elderberries! On that note, I think it is time for me to get back to work; and just so you know, I'm sorry I had to question you concerning Jude Prichart's death. I was just doing my job."

"I'm sorry I let go with that foulmouthed outburst," responded Cindy. "Can we agree to shake hands and start over?"

"Shake hands? Heck no! I want a hug, and no, I'm not trying to butter you up for a 'loan' in case you become filthy rich."

With unsteady legs, Cindy stood and gave the sheriff a hug. "I think we've buried the hatchet, but don't ask me for money," she said with a strained laugh.

After the sheriff left, Cindy sank into one of the living room chairs and gave in to feelings of disbelief threatening to overwhelm her. She talked to herself. "I can't believe Melvin left the bulk of his estate to me. I barely knew the man. I am the last person who knows how to go about building a first class five-star resort, let alone oversee the process and manage a restaurant. I don't even know where to begin. Josh is dead and can't offer advice. Damn you, Josh Morgan! Why didn't you listen to me when I tried to tell you there was nothing romantic going on between David Mercer and me when he was hospitalized? I was only there to help him quiet down. Instead, you chose to listen to that lying slut Ellie Montgomery! Look where it got you . . . a social disease and suicide when we could have had such a beautiful life together." She continued to sit there lost in thought when the afternoon sun faded into shades of dusk. There was no doubt she needed to talk with someone she trusted before any decisions were made. She wondered if that someone was David Mercer.

CHAPTER TWENTY-ONE

The evil influence of Sharon Murphy did not end with her arrest. She was determined to carry out what she started regarding the demise of David Mercer. In her mind it was too bad other men living in the house would have to be sacrificed, but so be it. Allowed the customary one phone call after being booked into the town jail, nobody would guess it wasn't to her attorney but to the individual she considered her closest friend, Audrey Wetzel, a mousey little spinster in her late sixties. Audrey thrived on rumors and looked up to Sharon as a guardian angel who engaged in keeping morals of the town intact. As a result, she would do anything to help her cause. Sharon was aware of her hold over the woman. She didn't hesitate to use that hold.

"Audrey it's me, Sharon. Don't talk, just listen. I have been booked into the town jail . . . that's what I just said . . . the town jail . . . It was NOT for propositioning the sheriff! HOW DARE YOU THINK SUCH A DISGUSTING THOUGHT! You know I would never do such a thing! . . . Oh, you were joking. Not funny! I was brought here to face charges for allegedly arranging the house to be burned where David Mercer and his group of misfits live . . . You heard right! I'm sorry to say that didn't happen. Our friend Rex chickened out and alerted the sheriff and Mercer . . . Yes, it was a stupid move on my part to go there, but I wanted to make sure Rex did what needed to be done . . . stop interrupting and listen, damn it! That means we go to plan B. When? Tonight, you idiot! Surely you haven't forgotten our discussions regarding plan B. Nobody will expect a repeat attempt tonight. Since I'm the primary suspect, I'll be in jail, so they can't accuse me. This could be my ticket out of here if you carry out plan B. Do not argue! Who would suspect someone like you? The supplies and instructions you will need are in the basement of my house . . . Stop that infernal blubbering! You know where to find the house key. You will do as I say or else! Even though you are my friend, you know what I'm capable of doing when people, even a friend like you, does not do as I say!" Sharon hung up and smiled to herself. "Guard! I'm ready to return to my cell," she gleefully announced, knowing Audrey would carry out her wishes.

The same Sunday morning as the attempted arson, Cindy decided to call David to explain her absence at church services. He assured her she didn't need to explain. He hadn't made it to church either. "I am calling you this morning to see if you and your friends are okay, and to ask if all of you would like to come out to my house for barbequed chicken and one of my almost famous chocolate cakes for dinner this evening." said Cindy "You would. That's great! See all of you around seven. Would it be possible for you to come early, around six? Why? I need to run something past you before I make a big decision about what to do next . . . I am positive I want your opinion, or I would not ask! I trust your judgment. Please don't ask for details now, and no, you do not need to bring anything except a healthy appetite and your thinking cap. See you then. Bye."

David groaned. He knew what the subject would be after what the sheriff told him regarding Melvin's will. He was also acutely aware he was not equipped to offer an opinion. After Cindy's call he immediately opened the door to his bedroom and shouted for everyone to meet in the living room.

"This is getting to be a habit," groused Larry, one of the men.

"Don't tell me you got a tip someone is planning to torch this rat trap again? That Murphy woman is in jail, and I can't think of anyone else who would want us dead," said Joe.

"Don't be so negative," said David. "Cindy called to invite all of us to her house for dinner. She is a good cook, so I don't expect the barbequed chicken or chocolate cake to be anything but wonderful. Do any of you have an objection to a good homecooked meal? There are leftover bologna sandwiches in the fridge if you choose to decline." Nobody voiced objections. "The rest of you need to plan on being there at seven. I plan to go a little earlier. She said there is something she wants to discuss with me." That comment brought catcalls and crude comments of a sexual nature, much to David's embarrassment. "Cool it! Cindy isn't that type of woman and I'm in no hurry to rush into . . . "

"Tell us another story we might believe," interjected another roommate, John. "It's easy to see you've fallen hard for her. What I don't understand is why she wants to see you before we get there. It would make more sense if she wanted you to stay after the rest of us leave."

David frowned. "I told you she isn't that kind of woman!"

"That's not what I heard. I heard she shacked up with that architect guy before he up and left town after coming down with some sort of social disease. Man, you're asking for trouble if you crawl into bed with her!"

"Where did you hear Cindy and I were being intimate, John?" asked an obviously upset David.

"I heard Sharon Murphy talking to a waitress at the deli."

"And you believe Sharon after what she tried to have done to this house, not to mention you are willing to go to Cindy's house for dinner? Shame on you! I've gotten to know her. She doesn't deserve those rumors!" exclaimed David. His response brought an apology from John. "I accept your apology, but don't ever let me hear you or any of the rest of you repeat those rumors, or there will be hell to pay!" David hotly declared.

David arrived at Cindy's house at six p.m. as she asked. "Hello pretty lady," he said as soon as she opened the front door. "You look unsettled. Care to let me know why? But first how about a hug?"

Cindy motioned him inside and closed the door before accepting his embrace. "The sheriff was here earlier this morning," she began. David frowned to give the impression he was unaware of what the sheriff told her.

"Don't tell me he is still trying to harass you about Jude Pritchard's death?"

"No, quite the opposite. He came bearing news regarding Melvin Prendergast," she replied.

"Wasn't he a wealthy car dealership, real estate broker and nightclub owner who shot himself after he killed his secretary and nephew? What could the sheriff possibly want from you? I thought it was a foregone conclusion Melvin was the culprit after the suicide note and what I witnessed and swore to in a deposition." David made these statements to give himself time to come up with a response before Cindy divulged why she wanted his opinion concerning the will.

"According to the sheriff, everyone thought the will was settled. This was before the cleaning crew working at Melvin's office found a will dated after the one his wife Betty produced," said Cindy.

"What does that have to do with you?" asked David.

"You aren't going to believe what I'm about to tell you." Cindy paused to take a deep breath before she could continue. "Melvin had another will made replacing the first one shortly before he shot himself. He . . . he left his estate to me."

David sat back in his chair without speaking for several minutes. He did this even though he was aware of the new will. "What prompted him to do that?" he finally asked.

"I don't know. I hardly knew the man. My contacts with him consisted of a brief hello after church or on those few occasions when we crossed paths at the deli, gas station or grocery store. He once mentioned he was sorry his former wife, Betty, and Sharon Murphy made nasty comments about me. I laughed it off, telling him not to worry about it, since they were not the only ones who had made such comments."

"Why are you telling me this?" inquired David.

"There are stipulations as to how the money is used. I'm not sure I am qualified to carry them out. I trust your opinion. I can't say that about a lot of people," replied Cindy.

"I'm flattered. What are the stipulations?"

"I am to use the money to build an upscale resort including a golf course, spa, pool, cabanas, hotel and restaurant on one hundred acres he owned on the north end of the lake," replied Cindy. "The name of the restaurant is to be Gracie's. If you recall, Grace was Melvin's secretary before he murdered her. I am assuming he wanted the restaurant named for her to ease his feelings of guilt for taking her life."

"Wow! Building all of that will take some big bucks!" was all David could say.

"To be precise, it will take $156.5 billion bucks for starters, and that's if his ex-wife doesn't contest the will and attorneys on both sides don't each end up with at least one third of the amount should she take that course of action."

"That means a lot of work and stress. What's in it for you?" asked David.

"If I walk away, I am to receive twenty-five grand. No strings attached. Town fathers get the rest to move forward with Melvin's plans and deal with Betty."

"What happens if you decide to go ahead with stipulations in the will?"

"Twenty-five thousand dollars free and clear, in addition to a guaranteed two thousand dollars a month from receipts of the restaurant as the manager, plus ten percent of all sales, including those of hotel, resort activities, spa and the golf course."

"Do you know anything about managing an upscale resort or for that matter, overseeing the building of such a resort?" asked David.

"Not a clue beyond watching this house being built, whipping up a few meals and baking cakes and cookies for friends and church bake sales," replied Cindy.

"I see your plight," replied David. "I don't see how I can give the kind of advice you need, but I will sleep on it, then I can get advice from people who do know what such an enterprise would require." Their conversation ended by the sound of knocking at the door. "Looks like I'm saved by my roomies," quipped David after jumping up to take a quick look through the peep hole to see who was there. "It's the guys. Would you like for me to open the door?"

"If you wouldn't mind, I'm sure the chicken needs my attention," replied Cindy. "Just herd the troops to the picnic table out back under the maple tree. Please grab the bowl of potato salad from the refrigerator on your way out the back door. Baked beans are already out there, along with biscuits in the grill warming oven."

"What, no chocolate cake?" questioned David.

"Take a look when you get out back. I think you will find two of them," answered Cindy.

The evening went far better than Cindy or David and his roommates expected while pretending they didn't know about the will. One lone chicken leg of five chickens Cindy barbequed survived the ravenous appetites of those present. The cooler filled with soft drinks empty, they all declared they could not eat another bite before agreeing it was time to go home, including David. He would have liked to linger a while but felt unprepared for the merciless teasing he would get from the others if he stayed behind after they left, not to mention the impact on Cindy's reputation in the event Sharon or one of her friends became aware of his being there to enjoy a homemade dinner.

Arriving a block from the halfway house, David and his buddies were surprised to find the street blocked off. Plumes of acrid-smelling smoke filled the air. An officer standing in front of sawhorses blocking the road raised his hand to stop both cars. David, in the lead car, rolled down his window to ask what the holdup was. "Sorry folks, you can't go any farther. There has been some sort of an explosion halfway up the block," he explained. "Sheriff's orders are to allow no one closer than these barricades for safety reasons."

"But we live on this block," argued David.

"I'm sorry, but you must wait until the fire department has everything under control. Until then please wait beside the curb until I get an all clear from the fire chief allowing you to proceed," insisted the officer. David nodded and gave the other car's driver the high sign to park his car curbside and he did the same.

All seven men piled out of the cars to wait for further instructions. "I wonder what happened?" questioned David.

Two hours later he would have an answer when the sheriff approached wearing a grim expression.

"I hate to be the bearer of bad news. The house where you guys live has been destroyed, along with severe damage to houses on either side. This is in addition to busted windows in the houses across and down the street. Four elderly neighbors, two on each side of what was your house, are presumed dead."

"Oh shit! What happened?" they all said in unison.

"We don't know for sure, but a natural gas leak is suspected," replied the sheriff.

"No houses in this area have natural gas. They are all electric," replied David.

"How would you know?" questioned the sheriff.

"We've all been guests for meals in adjoining houses and those across the street. We know they are all electric just like the one where we live," responded David.

"Guess that answers one of a lot of questions," replied the sheriff. "The next question is, can one of you identify remains of people living on either side of your house?" The men remained silent as they studied the ground. "I will," volunteered David. "You know we all suffer from military related PTSD, don't you?" The sheriff confirmed with a nod then David continued. "This is not going to be easy. I am asking you to contact Cindy Marsh to stand by after viewing of the bodies is completed. She was very adept at helping me manage my symptoms while I was a patient at the hospital. I'm sure she can be of help to me and any of the other men who have problems."

"That can be arranged as soon as I can get to a phone," agreed the sheriff. "I forgot to charge mine."

"Here, you can use mine," offered David, handing him his cell phone. "Then again, maybe it's best if I go back to her house and ask for her help personally. All of us left there two hours ago after having dinner with her."

"If you don't think knocking on her door this late will scare the hell out of her, go ahead. But you need to be aware she has a gun and knows how to use it," said the sheriff.

"You're right. I should call first. She may be annoyed being awakened, but the heads up will give her time to recover before I get there," agreed David. The sheriff handed David's phone back to him.

"Get on with it!" demanded one of the men irritably. "We've got to find somewhere to sleep tonight and the longer you take, the harder it will be to find a place." David took the not-too gentle hint and hit the button for Cindy's phone number on his cell phone.

"Lo," answered Cindy thickly. "Whoever you are it had better be important!"

"It's me," replied David. "I hate calling so late, but my friends and I have a problem."

The urgent tone of his voice caused Cindy to sit upright and turn on the bedside lamp. "Please don't tell me you were in an accident on the way home!"

"I'm afraid it's worse. The house where we've been living has been destroyed by an explosion, along with severe damage to houses on either side of us. Windows are shattered in houses across and down the street." David made the decision to hold back letting her know their immediate neighbors on either side had been killed.

Fear gripped her. "Oh my god! What happened? Are all of you alright?" she exclaimed.

"The explosion and resulting fire happened before we arrived on the scene, so none of us were hurt. But we lost everything we own except the clothes we are wearing. We have nowhere to go, at least tonight. Would it be possible for us to stay with you?"

"It's a relief to know none of you were hurt. All of you need to come to my house. You know there are three guest rooms in addition to the master bedroom and a sofa bed in the den. You are all welcome to stay here as long as necessary," Cindy offered without hesitation. David gave a thumbs up to the men uneasily milling around listening to the one-sided conversation. "Thanks for the offer, Cindy, but are you sure you want all of us? You do realize there could be problems with the stress this is causing?" cautioned David.

"I'm sure. You are all welcome. I learned a great deal how to deal with PTSD, thanks to you. Don't forget, you have recovered enough to help me if anyone decides to go ballistic. I'll put on the coffee pot, make that a pot of hot chocolate, and get a plate of cookies ready. I have no doubt at least some of the guys will need to calm down. Serving caffeine-loaded coffee would make it more difficult for that to happen."

"Hot chocolate is a good idea. What will we do in the morning about serving breakfast to seven hungry men?" asked David.

"One thing at a time," she replied. "We'll worry about breakfast when the time comes. Managing tonight is important in that all of you need to unwind then get some sleep."

David agreed. "See you soon, and thanks again." He turned to his buddies while continuing to keep Cindy on the line so she could hear what he said to them. "It's going to be alright. Cindy wants us to come back to her house and spend the night. We all know this town can be a hotbed for rumors, but many people living here band together and lend a helping hand when there has been a disaster. I believe what happened tonight qualifies as a disaster."

"Speaking of disaster, do the authorities have any idea what caused the explosion?" shouted Cindy into her cell phone.

"Not at this time, although the sheriff seems to think there could be some sort of chemically induced explosion," replied David.

"What kind of chemical explosion?" she questioned. David was becoming rattled by her questioning. "Can we talk about this when we get to your house? The guys are restless. I don't want anyone going ape on me during the drive to your place," he pleaded.

"Sure thing," replied Cindy, already in the process of getting out of her nightgown into a t-shirt, jeans and tennis shoes to be ready to deal with the aftermath of them losing everything with few options of what will happen in the future. *This explosion may not have been an accident*, she thought. *But who would do such a thing after what Sharon tried to do by ordering the fire less than 24 hours ago? How could Sharon be responsible? She's in jail.* Still, Cindy could not help thinking Sharon was somehow involved in what took place.

CHAPTER TWENTY-TWO

At the site of destroyed houses, fire marshal Simon Hollister was concluding his preliminary investigation amid grumblings. In his mind, he was called out of bed to come to the scene at what he considered an ungodly hour. Sheriff Heinz apologized but reminded Simon he had no choice since there was evidence involving four dead people in adjoining houses on either side of the initial explosion. "Sorry to call you out here at this hour Simon, but with four bodies we've found on either side of the initial location, you know I didn't have a choice."

"It's a good thing you called. I found a fifth body, or what little remains of it, just inside the back door of the primary location under what appears to be part of the roof that didn't burn or get blown to bits," replied Simon. "There is no doubt in my mind this mess is the result of this person setting off some sort of an explosive device. The perp wasn't smart enough to allow time for him or her to escape after detonating the device. This indicates it wasn't a professional hit. I'll feel sure after forensic tests are completed and we know what of type of materials were used to construct the bomb. Looks like you need to call the coroner and get him out here as soon as possible. Be sure to tell him he will need five body bags, not four."

"Have you met the new county coroner?" asked the sheriff.

"Can't say as I have," replied the fire marshal.

"You are in for a real treat. She's the kind of woman you don't tell what to do," replied the sheriff.

"Is that so? I'll just have to see about that," he scoffed.

"Don't say I didn't warn you. I think you just might meet your match. That's all I'm going to say beyond good luck." *You are going to need it*, thought the sheriff. *Once you get a load of the way she's built and the hair on her upper lip, arms and legs you just might think you've met the female version of sasquatch with temperament to match!*

"What are you smiling about?" asked Simon with a scowl. "We are standing not ten feet away from what appears to be a case of arson and the remains of five dead bodies, so wipe that smile off your face and get this crowd of people back into their houses before someone gets hurt!" he barked. The sheriff apologized and told him he sometimes tended to smile when under stress. "Yeah, at one of those state required sensitivity meetings, I learned that can happen," Simon replied with an increasing scowl meant to convey he wasn't buying it.

Asleep on her jail cell bunk, Sharon Murphy awakened to muted sounds of an explosion followed by sirens. She turned over, a smile on her face, thinking Audrey had done as she was told. Any future problems with David Mercer and his friends were solved. She felt confident it would be only a matter of time before a jury found her not guilty of arranging arson of the halfway house, murder or attempted murder in charge associated with Cindy's elderberry pie. She mistakenly believed the statute of limitation had expired on the poisoned pie she fed her husband, but that is not true when murder is involved. She also felt confident people seated on the jury would fear having their secrets revealed and end up acquitting her of all charges. Resisting the urge to laugh out loud, she could only imagine the degree of chaos happening should she start telling everyone's secrets in a crowded courtroom of onlookers, including members of the news media and church attendees.

CHAPTER TWENTY-THREE

It was barely seven a. m. the day following the explosion. Cindy, awakened by loud knocking on her front door, could only hope it didn't disturb the sleeping men. She groaned and turned over in her comfortable bed, pulling the covers up around her neck. "I don't know who is knocking, but if I don't answer the door maybe they will go away." The knocking persisted, causing her to groan louder. "Guess I need to get up and go see who is causing all this ruckus," she muttered. Slipping into a robe and slippers, she made her way down the hall into the living room to peek out from behind the curtained window located beside the front door. There stood what she estimated to be twenty people, all with baskets, bags or boxes in hand. She recognized most of them from church.

Marie Saunders saw her peeking around the curtains and shouted, "Hey Cindy. Open the door! These boxes and baskets are getting heavy! A couple more minutes and you are going to be cleaning raw eggs off your porch, not to mention boiled potatoes and sides of ham ready for frying in cast iron skillets!" Cindy opened the door to find a flood of people entering and willing to lend a hand. "I don't know what to say," she blurted.

"*Thank you* would be a good start," said one of the men. "You want me to wake up those lazy loafers and tell them to get their butts out of bed? Or should I get my bugle from the truck and blow revelry? I hear tell they are all retired military."

"Please don't do either one," begged Cindy. "They all suffer from PTSD. Loud sounds could set them off, not to mention they had a rough night." The man grimaced and looked crestfallen while mumbling an apology. "I'm sure you didn't know," assured Cindy as she patted his arm. "Just knock softly on the bedroom doors and tell them breakfast will be ready in less than an hour." She pointed the way to the bedrooms. The man did as he was asked without further comments.

David was first to enter the living room wearing the same clothes he had worn last night, minus shoes. His usually combed hair was mussed. He needed a shave, but his ready but tired smile caught the attention of several women, just as it did for his roommates when they began appearing in much the same condition. It did not take long before everyone was drinking coffee, filling paper plates with food and talking about happenings of the previous night. Occasionally, nervous, muted laughter could be heard. The meal progressed with many people sitting cross-legged on the living room.

When everyone had eaten his or her fill, Miranda Jefferies, the bank vice-president, stood and started tapping a knife against her coffee cup in a vain effort to silence everyone. "May I have your attention, please?" she said in a normal voice. When that did not give the silence she needed, she yelled, "SHUT THE HELL UP!" The room became quiet, and she smiled. "That's more like it. We need to come up with a plan to help these guys. They lost everything. Cindy can't be expected to host them for what could become days or weeks before adequate housing is found, let alone feed these hungry hound dogs." That comment brought laughter and several howls. "I think they would have eaten eggshells if we hadn't hustled them out the back door to the compost pile!" This brought gales of more nervous laughter from everyone present. By now it was known this was where Sharon's poisoned pie ended up. "I need three, make it four, volunteers to help me come up with a plan. If you are wondering why four people, that gives an odd number when you count me. I refuse to deal with a large group where majority doesn't rule." A dozen hands shot up. She selected four, two women and two men. "We will meet on the front porch after we clean up the kitchen."

Cindy spoke up. "The guys can all stay here if you will help feed them, supply clothing, donate personal care items and volunteer to do some laundry each week." Miranda told her to consider it done.

Despite chaos in the ensuing days, Cindy gave consideration concerning a decision about what she needed to do next—not only concerning the men and their wellbeing, but also about the money Melvin Pendergast willed to her. During the time David spent there, he and Cindy held many conversations, both pro and con. Neither of them wanted to admit it, but they began developing serious feelings for each other. Especially at bedtime. They each took the high road to end up in separate bedrooms. Both knew something had to give, but which one would make the first move was still up for grabs.

CHAPTER TWENTY-FOUR

Everyone in the entire town and county vied for seats in the courthouse the day the Sharon Murphy trial was slated to begin with jury selection. Well, not quite everyone. Several prominent men of the community found it necessary to be "out of town on important business" should Sharon decide to spill her guts concerning illicit affairs if any one of them should be selected as a member of the jury. Individuals receiving summons to serve responded, except for the heretofore mentioned men. They gave various excuses to not serve, such as, "I will be out of the country on business," or, "I'm taking care of my dying grandmother," etc. This left the judge no recourse except to excuse them over the objections of Sharon. She felt none of them would find her guilty for fear their misdeeds would be exposed. She became so loud and obnoxious, the judge threatened to duct tape her mouth shut or remove her from the courtroom. Her court appointed attorney asked for a ten-minute recess to calm her down, which was swiftly granted.

Judge Wiley Preston Phillips III was nervous about being the presiding judge. He was not sure if Sharon knew about his one-night stand with the court stenographer. That was until he remembered he had the power of the almighty gavel and would not hesitate to use it to silence Sharon by having her taken from the room if the subject came come up. He could not help wondering if such action would be swift enough before she made the liaison known. Wiping perspiration from his forehead with his hand, he decided to take the chance. Otherwise, it would be months before another judge could be found willing to preside.

On the first day, thirty prospective jurors milled around in a small adjoining room to drink lukewarm, weak coffee in white Styrofoam cups. The portly bailiff came into the area and called out the names of each person to be questioned, then placed a checkmark beside each name on his clipboard. Much to her horror, a matronly woman's name was then called. "Mabel Reeves, come with me."

Mabel happened to be the wife of one of the men who asked to be excused due to pressing business. Dressed in her Sunday best, a dark blue, full-skirted number with a white lace collar and strand of fake pearls, she stood before the judge. The bailiff asked her to raise her right hand and swear on the bible there was no reason why she should not be a juror. By the time the prosecuting and Sharon's attorney voiced multiple protests during their questioning amid her vague answers, she was in tears. This left Sharon's attorney, Beecher Calvin McDonald, Esq. to insist Mabel be dismissed. The judge overruled his request, along with a reminder that Sharon (who shouted repeatedly during the questioning) must remain silent or speak only to her attorney in a normal tone of voice, or she would be removed from the proceedings. Glaring coldly at the judge she complied. Before noon lunch recess, all but three jurors summoned were dismissed with cause. This meant another round of potential jurors must be summoned delaying the trial. This is when Sharon's attorney approached the bench to ask Sharon be released on her own recognizance pending final jury selection. "Go ahead, plead your case," the judge replied.

"Your Honor, Mrs. Murphy is a prominent member of this community," he began. "Why, her father helped found this town." (Not true.) "She attends church services every Sunday, rain or shine. I am asking she be released on her own recognizance or minimal bond until such time as a jury is seated, the trial is completed and she is found innocent of all charges," pleaded the sweating man. He crossed his fingers behind his back and silently begged God to forgive him for asking for such consideration. Sharon sat ramrod straight dressed in the faded blue jumpsuit with the word INMATE stenciled in black across the back and front. Her ankles were crossed and her hands were clasped in her lap while she desperately tried to look like a picture of pure innocence. The attorneys' plea did not work.

"Mrs. Murphy will remain in custody until such time a jury of her peers finds her guilty or innocent," ordered the judge.

"Mr. Phillips, as a member of the bar, I'm sure you are aware charges of alleged arson resulting in death and attempted murder do not afford the luxury of bail, regardless of personal recognizance." The judge's gavel hitting the benchtop ended the conversation. The attorney slinked back to his seat.

"Court is dismissed until next Monday at nine a.m. or another round of jurors can be provided, examined and sworn in," declared the judge. "Bailiff, you may escort Mrs. Murphy back to her cell." This is when the judge knew it was do or die; either Sharon knew about his one-night stand, or she didn't. To his relief she only began to swear and make it difficult for the bailiff to put her hands back into handcuffs. Twisting and turning, she forced the bailiff to bring in two additional deputies to subdue her, but not without bruises, scratches and threats to reveal their secrets.

It took two additional weeks to interview sixty more prospective jurors in order to seat a jury composed of five women and four men. This happened after the defense attorney failed to have the trial moved to Portland. "I tried, really I tried," pleaded Mr. Phillips when Sharon began to curse him to the extent the judge had her removed from the courtroom and fined one hundred dollars for contempt. After looking at his calendar, he announced the trial would begin the first Monday in in June in Riverwood, six weeks from that day. "Sorry folks, but with me being a circuit judge for three counties, my docket is full until then." Neither Sharon nor her attorney were happy with the delay.

The prosecuting attorney found himself struggling whether he should share damning evidence provided by a letter written by Audrey Wetzel. His lack of action could result in an appeal or disbarment in the event Sharon was found guilty if he waited to present it as evidence. He finally decided to wait, telling himself he would release the letter only if there was not enough other collaborating evidence to find Sharon guilty, plead he had just received it from an unknown source, and hope the judge believed him; this course of action was based on his feeling sorry for Audrey and what the letter would do to her reputation.

Unfortunately, or fortunately when the trial got underway, Prosecutor Parsons was able to read the faces of jury members when David Mercer and Cindy Marsh gave their testimonies. There was no doubt it would be necessary for him to reveal Audrey Wetzel's letter. Members of the jury had done little to hide contempt of both Cindy and David based on subtle remarks made repeatedly by Sharon's attorney regarding Cindy and her relationship with David and his roommates.

"They are both lying! That March woman is nothing but a whore!" screamed Sharon. Her actions got her removed from the courtroom and another fine for contempt amid gasps and twitters among onlookers.

The judge banged his gavel. "We will take a ten-minute recess. Jurors will disregard any statements made by the defendant or members of the audience," he announced before addressing the audience. "When we resume, there will be order in this courtroom or all of you, with the exception of those needed to perform duties associated with this trial, will be removed!" Everyone fell silent, and nobody moved except the judge, who retired to his chambers. Silence prevailed when he returned to the bench and appeared stern. The bailiff instructed the audience to stand by, saying, "All rise." His Honor took his elevated seat and stated all could be seated. The trial resumed.

CHAPTER TWENTY-FIVE

Two weeks passed before motel rooms were available for Josh and his friends at minimal cost. Clothing and personal supplies started rolling in from all over the tri-county area. The inn's owner found it necessary to place a sign in the front window asking everyone to hold off bringing more supplies until he placed another sign listing specifically what was needed. In a matter of days, David and his friends became celebrities with offers to appear on TV talk shows and radio stations based in Portland and Seattle. They declined, giving only brief, vague statements to the weekly Riverwood newspaper editor.

Three former veterans signed on for deputy training with the sheriff's department. The others, including David, began hanging out during the day doing chores, watching TV, reading or napping at Cindy's house. If she had any thoughts of facing a long cold winter alone, she was wrong. Christmas and New Year's Eve found her house to be party central including David, his buddies and many of those who lent helping hands following the explosion. After the holidays, six young ladies began arriving on a regular basis at what she later learned was by invitation of David's buddies. She made it clear there would not be overnight stays despite groans indicating displeasure of those involved. "While all of you are visiting in my home, you will abide by my rules, or you can find arrangements elsewhere," she declared. Despite this declaration, the socializing led to more ridiculous rumors by Sharon's few remaining cronies who had not been invited to attend the parties. Rumors included that Cindy was now operating a house of ill repute. To squelch those rumors, the church pastor, at great risk to his job, gave a sermon on how rumors can destroy people's lives. He could have saved his breath for all the good it did. In a show of contempt for rumors, Cindy and David decided to attend church on a regular basis, going so far as to linger outside on the sidewalk following each service. This maneuver forced people to acknowledge them or step aside into wet and sometimes muddy grass.

CHAPTER TWENTY-SIX

Cindy made the decision to table further discussions with David or the town fathers regarding Melvin Pendergast's will until Sharon Murphy's trial ended. This decision became more critical than she imagined when people started voicing concerns as to the whereabouts of Audrey Wetzel. The spinster had not been seen in public since weeks before the trial began. A search of her home produced no sign of her. Prosecutor Harry Parsons knew it was time to reveal Audrey's letter and hoped the judge did not give him any trouble. It was with trembling hands he asked permission that he and the defendant's council meet in chambers. His mouth became dry as the judge gave permission and silently read the letter's content through bifocals perched on the tip of his nose. The letter read as follows:

November 3, 2020

Dear Mr. Parsons,

I am having this letter delivered to you in case something goes wrong. Sharon Murphy threatened me with deadly harm if I didn't assemble and deliver the bomb that blew up the house where David Mercer and his friends live. Should I disappear or die in the blast, I don't want this on my conscience without asking for forgiveness. I am truly really very sorry. I hope all of you and God will forgive me for being weak.

Sincerely,

Audrey Wetzel

"Why in the hell have you waited until now to present this letter dated the day of the explosion into evidence? Explain yourself Harry!" roared Judge Prescott. Sharon's attorney echoed the same question.

"The letter was just delivered to me last night," lied Mr. Parsons.

"And who delivered it?" demanded the judge.

"I don't know Your Honor," replied Harry. "I found it slipped under my front door when I arrived home late last night."

"If I didn't know you to be an honest man, I would toss you in jail for withholding critical information," replied the Judge. "It is the ruling of this court you must give a copy to the defense immediately since final proceedings were to have started in one hour. The original letter will become state's evidence. Court will recess for three days giving the defense time to read its copy and decide what course of action it will take. I am also ruling the prosecution must hire a professional handwriting expert who will be summoned to testify to the fact Andrey Wetzel wrote and signed this letter. This court is in recess until nine a. m. three days from today!"

All hell broke loose among onlookers when court reconvened, and the letter was introduced into evidence. Sharon added to the melee by shouting, "I have my rights! I demand to see the letter right now! Audrey would never have betrayed me!" she insisted, not realizing her protests could be interpreted as a confession.

The judge pounded his gavel, shouting for order. "I will have order in this court room! Bailiff, clear this room immediately! Jurors will remain seated until the courtroom is cleared. Jurors, you are hereby instructed not to discuss this case with anyone, watch television news reports, listen to the radio or read any newspaper accounts under penalty of law! You will not take under consideration any outburst made by the defendant or onlookers. Mrs. Murphy, your attorney will show you a copy of the letter when you next meet in your cell to discuss your case."

That said, Judge Prescot slammed his gavel on the benchtop, rose and made an exit through the door located behind the bench into his office. Once inside, he shed his black robe and reached for the bottle of whiskey kept hidden in the bottom desk drawer. Instead of looking for a glass he took several swigs straight from the bottle. "I should have become an accountant like my parents wanted me to," he said into the empty room.

Over lunch with David at the deli, Cindy asked why the trial had been delayed since she did not linger after giving her testimony.

"I don't have any more of an idea than you," he replied. "We were separated and neither of us allowed in the courtroom prior to our testimony since we are both prosecution witnesses, so I didn't stick around either. In fact, it probably isn't a good idea we are seen having lunch together. Somebody might get the idea we are comparing stories, even though we've already testified—someone like Thelma Jenkins sitting at the next table." He made this statement loudly enough that Thelma blushed and lowered her head as though examining her salad for foreign objects. "We need to eat and get out of here as soon as possible. You go home. I will go to my hotel room," said David, this time loudly enough he was sure Thelma could hear what he said without question.

Later that afternoon, word spread, compliments of Thelma Jenkins, Cindy was headed to David's hotel room to engage in immoral activities, and the judge should be alerted the two of them were overheard comparing stories of what had happened in order to make Sharon Murphy look bad, and they should both be cross examined again. The judge, after receiving several phone calls from Sharon's friends, refused to believe or act on the rumor.

The following Sunday morning, another sermon was delivered by the preacher involving the sin of spreading rumors. Thelma Jenkins slipped out the church back door instead of shaking the pastor's hand while exiting the narthex to tell him what a good sermon he had delivered, as she would normally have done. Later in the coming week, the pastor was not at all surprised when he was called before the church Board of Trustees and asked for his immediate resignation. When asked why, he was told there had been numerous complaints he was much too focused on denouncing rumors when he should be preaching hell and brimstone.

CHAPTER TWENTY-SEVEN

A week later, following two days of testimony, including verification of Audrey Wetzel letter and signature by an expert, the jury deliberated only three hours before returning with their verdict. "What say you?" asked the judge.

Jury foreman Mandy Robertson stood, with her hands shaking as she read from the prepared statement. "We the jury find the defendant, Sharon Murphy, guilty of murder in the first degree and attempted murder as charged." She read the verdict without looking in Sharon's direction.

Sharon gasped and would have stood, but her legs would not allow it. This did not stop her from hurling insults at Mandy and other members of the jury. "All of you sitting on the jury are nothing but trash! You, Mandy, are among the worst! I know what you do when your husband is out of town . . ."

The judge stopped her from continuing while banging his gavel to maintain order. "You will hold your tongue, Mrs. Murphy! Bailiff, remove Mrs. Murphy from the courtroom immediately and get her back to her cell! Sentencing will happen one month from today," he declared before thanking members of the jury for their time and dismissing them.

Members of the press were waiting to speak to jurors when they exited the courthouse. "Why did you take only three hours to reach a verdict?" demanded one reporter. "You do realize by finding Mrs. Murphy guilty of murder and attempted murder she could be sentence to life in prison? And that is the same as death at her advanced age?"

"We found her guilty after hearing testimony from Cindy and David, the letter written by Audrey Wetzel and lab reports pertaining to arsenic in the pie Sharon gave Cindy," replied one of the male members of the jury.

"There was never doubt in any of our minds she is guilty as charged," echoed another, a female.

"Is that so? It seems odd you can name the full name of the writer of the letter, but you refer only to the first name of two key witnesses. Are you sure this jury was impartial? I've heard rumors Mrs. Murphy was in possession of information which could cause embarrassment to most of you seated on the jury! Did you see finding her guilty a means of getting her out of the picture?" After those statements, jury members declined any more comments as they silently pushed past members of the press and quickly walked to their respective cars.

Nobody was surprised when the local newspaper featured the headline, "SHARON MURPHY FOUND GUILTY OF MURDER!" The article went on to say sentencing would happen in a month. This was in addition to words Sharon shouted upon hearing the jury's verdict, many of which were blacked out. The Portland and Seattle newspapers had a field day, as did TV and radio stations.

The morning after the trial Cindy and David sat drinking coffee while seated at her front deck patio table. "Boy, am I glad that's over!" declared David. "I hope Sharon gets the maximum allowed by law."

"I can't see the judge doing anything less," replied Cindy. The words were hardly out of her mouth when a carload of men came to a screeching halt in front of the house to start shouting. "Hey there Cindy baby! Looks like you and David got away with murder! Too bad your luck didn't carry over to Sharon. We heard about the deal David had with Sharon to shut her up by kicking her out of her house. Had that not happened she wouldn't have found it necessary for arrangements to have you and your friends killed. What do you have to say about that?" demanded the car's driver.

"Yeah, what about it?" questioned another man.

"Let's go inside," said David. "We don't have to sit out here listening to these idiots!"

"You realize they will keep coming back to sling more insults, don't you?" replied Cindy.

"Maybe so, but today I'm not in any frame of mind to deal rationally with the likes of them." They both picked up their coffee cups and calmly walked into the house, shutting the door behind them. When it became apparent Cindy and David refused to interact with their tormentors, the tormenters sped away.

Once seated at the kitchen table, Cindy nervously wrapped and unwrapped her hands around her coffee cup while gathering courage to speak. "David, we need to talk. What were those guys referring to when they mentioned the deal you had with Sharon? I thought we didn't have secrets between us."

"I know," replied David. "First, I need to know how you feel about me. I made it clear earlier that I'm in love with you and want to marry you. At the same time, I'm not sure you have those feeling for me since you haven't told me how you feel."

Cindy didn't know how to answer his question. She knew she felt deep affection for David, but marriage was another matter. They had been through a lot together, but love and marriage? That was something needing more thought. It was such an important decision. Her hesitation to his question said more than words could say. Without answering her question concerning the deal with Sharon, David got up and started to leave.

"David," she pleaded. "I said we need to talk." Instead of pausing, he brushed passed her, walked out the door onto the porch and went down the steps toward his truck. "I don't think there is anything to talk about right now. Be sure to lock your doors," he shouted over his shoulder before climbing into his truck to drive away.

Cindy stood in the open doorway and watched David's truck drive out of sight. "What have I done?" she lamented. "He has been my rock during our shared ordeals. At the same time, I need more time to make sure I'm making the right decisions, not only concerning our future, but what to do about the inheritance from Melvin . . . David doesn't know the town's mayor managed to find out about the will demanding I decide in next few days or he, along with Melvin's former wife, plan to file lawsuits to have the will overturned. This is what I wanted to discuss with David tonight, and now he left thinking I don't care about him. Plus, he didn't answer my question concerning the details of his deal with Sharon Murphy. This reminds me of what happened with Josh when he refused to hear me out. I don't know what to do!"

Her laments were interrupted by the same carload of men stopping in front of her house again. "Hey Cindy!

Where's the old guy you've been bonking? The truck's gone. What's the matter? Aren't you putting out tonight, or does he have another hot babe back in town? We would hate for you to spend a lonely evening. There are five of us who would like to keep you company. What about it, baby? A woman of your reputation can easily handle five studs like us in one night. What do you think?"

"I think you need to get the hell out of here!" she screamed. "I'm calling the sheriff.

"Don't tell me you got a thing going with him too? Why, that old codger probably hasn't had a hard on for the past twenty years, and you're telling five studs to hit the road?" yelled the driver.

Cindy did not answer. Instead, she got up, went inside the house to return with a loaded double barrel shotgun. Aiming then firing just above the car's roof got their attention. "Next time I will shoot lower, so get the hell out of here, and don't come back!" she screamed. The men wasted little time leaving. Back inside, Cindy sank down on the sofa and cried. "What am I going to do, God? I have lived my entire life here. I have never done anything bad or said anything untrue about anyone. I mind my own business and help anyone in need, yet I bear the brunt of these terrible rumors! Damn you to hell, Sharon Murphy! If it weren't for you, Ellie

Montgomery and your minions, my life would not be in such a mess!"

CHAPTER TWENTY-EIGHT

On the drive back to town, David knew he had blown it big time with Cindy. He pounded is right fist against his thigh. "I should not have pressured her to make a commitment. I should have stopped short of telling her I loved her and not asked how she felt about me. I don't blame her if she doesn't want anything more to do with me, and that breaks my heart." Not one to cry, David didn't realize what he thought was mist on the windshield were tears threatening to spill down his cheeks. Arriving at the motel he and his buddies were temporarily calling home after the fire, he merely waved to them on the way to his room as they sat in a cluster of lawn chairs drinking soda on the patio near the small swimming pool.

A few minutes later, Elmer and John pounded on his on his door. He did not respond as quickly as they thought he should. "Hey, David!" they yelled. Instead of answering, he went to the bathroom and splashed cold water on his face hoping it would remove red splotches, the result of his emotional state. "Be with you in a minute! Can't a guy take a leak without one of you pounding on my door!"

"That must be one heck of a piss," yelled John in response. "You been back for about ten minutes, make it twenty minutes. It's not like you to miss a chance to chew the fat and have a cold soda before going to bed for the night. What's the matter? Did Cindy kick you out early?" *If you only knew*, thought David. *My name will be mud when you guys learn she . . .* He could not finish the thought of how the guys would react once they learned there was a real chance he would no longer be welcomed with open arms at Cindy's house. His first impulse was to beg off joining them, saying he had a headache and wanted to go to bed. But he knew sooner or later he would have to answer questions, so he might as well join his friends for at least a few minutes.

"Are we all going to Cindy's tomorrow evening?" asked Elmer after Josh joined them. "Earlier today, she called to invite all of us for burgers and some of that delicious chocolate cake she makes from scratch."

Taken off guard by the comment, David hesitated before answering. "I was not aware she issued an invitation. I think I'll take a rain check. The rest of you feel free to go."

"I knew it!" declared John.

"You knew what?" asked David as he squirmed uncomfortably in his chair.

"You're home early looking like you lost your best friend. You two had a fight, didn't you?"

David stared intently at the ground. "It wasn't really a fight. I messed up."

"Okay, out with it! You are among friends. You know you can tell us anything," said Jake.

David got up from his chair. "I messed up. Just leave it at that! Can't a guy have a little privacy around here?" That said, he headed for his hotel room, slamming the door behind him. Startled by the unexpected response, his buddies became quiet then went to their respective rooms.

David spent a restless night talking to himself while tossing and turning. "I don't want to lose her. Cindy is the best thing that's happened to me since mustering out of the Marines. If it weren't for her, I would be a slobbering drunk or dead in some back alley or roadside ditch."

He had no idea that Cindy was also experiencing a restless night. "What is wrong with me? David is a great guy. What is stopping me from revealing my true feelings for him?" she muttered into her tear-dampened pillow. Deep in her heart she knew but did not want to appear weak and needy after having been rejected by Josh following the loss of her beloved Harold. Going through that kind of torment was more than she could bear again.

CHAPTER TWENTY-NINE

It was a sad group of men who arrived at Cindy's for burgers after debating whether to show up or call with a lame excuse why they could not attend. "We have to go," announced John. "It is the only way we are going to learn what happened since David isn't talking. We can't just sit by and let two people meant for each other end their relationship without at least trying to help."

All but Jake eventually agreed. "We don't need to go poking our noses into their private business. That's what is wrong with this damned town!" he announced with conviction.

"You have a point," declared John. "We agreed not be involved in rumors. We only have concern for two people who are dear friends. If Cindy doesn't want to tell us what happened, that will be the end of it but not before I tell David he is making a big mistake. If he doesn't apologize and try to make things right with her, I'm going to give him a swift kick in the pants!"

"How do you know what happened was his fault?" asked Rubin. "It takes two to make an argument. I say we go to find out the facts before we try to play Cupid. I don't know about the rest of you guys, but I'm not good at shooting a bow and arrow." This brought a few chuckles from the others before they agreed to go have burgers and a conversation with Cindy before any more decisions were made about what, or what not, to do to bring Cindy and David back together. "What do we tell Cindy when David doesn't show up?" questioned Rubin. Each man looked at the next for an answer that was not forthcoming until Jake spoke up again. "I don't think we need to say anything. Sometimes silence is the best answer."

Cindy was having second thoughts about asking David and roommates to her home for dinner. She knew there would be tension between her and David, and they would expect answers to questions she was not prepared to answer. It wasn't until the last possible moment she decided to go ahead and have the cookout.

CHAPTER THIRTY

Cindy was still feeling sorry she invited David and his friends for hamburgers. She was even more sorry when John called to say everyone except David would be there. Rather than disappoint the guys, she said she would look forward to seeing them, hoping she would not be questioned why David was not among them. The onions she was slicing had nothing to do with her tears while adding them to the plate of sliced tomatoes, dill pickles, lettuce and onions to garnish the burgers. *I must pull myself together before they get here*, she thought. I know, I will have a glass of white wine before they arrive. That will relax me. By the time one of the guys knocked on the door, she was all smiles and felt ready for their company with help from a second glass of wine. "At least with them here I will not have to cry alone for a couple of hours," she muttered before opening the door to greet them.

"Hello Cindy. Good to see you. Thanks for the invite," said Jake, the first one through the door after she answered. It did not take long before they all ended up out back under the maple tree seated at the picnic table, cans of soda in their hands. Hank took charge of grilling the burgers.

"Scuse me while I go inside and get the potato salad from the 'frigerator," Cindy slurred. It was easy to see she was unsteady on her feet, having imbibed in her fourth glass of wine in less than three hours, two of them just prior to arrival of her guests. Her condition did not go unnoticed by John, who followed closely enough to catch her should she fall on the uneven patio stones. Before she could open the kitchen screen door, John stepped in front of her to usher her inside with a sweep of his hand. His gallant gesture made her giggle. He knew this would be the perfect time to ask what had taken place between her and David without involving the other guys. Cindy's first reaction to John's gallantry and question was to continue giggling and ask what he meant before she burst into tears. "I messed up," she blubbered.

"That is the same thing David said," replied John. "Funny how you two seem to think alike. Would you care to elaborate how you messed up? David isn't talking. So, it's up to you to fill me in if there is anything me or the others can do to help both of you handle this misunderstanding. At least we will have a head start on what to do next." His comment, added to the amount of unaccustomed wine she had consumed, opened the flood gates. Cindy began to pour out her heart in addition to her tears. "David asked me to marry him. I said I would need time to think about an answer to such a serious proposal. Before he popped the question, I asked about the deal he had with Sharon, and he wouldn't give me an answer, saying that wasn't anything we needed to talk about. Then he abruptly left, thinking I don't care about him, when I do care. In fact, I love him, but marriage is a serious commitment, 'specially when both of us have a lot of baggage in our past."

John sighed and handed her a paper napkin to wipe her eyes and blow her nose. "I know about the deal David had with Sharon. He went to her house to confront her about rumors she was spreading about you. He didn't tell you Sharon is a cousin, did he?"

"No, he didn't," she replied.

"Well, she is, and at the request of his dying mother, David promised to allow Sharon to continue living in the house she and his father owned here in Riverwood as a retreat. Sharon thought she inherited the house when her husband died, but that was not true. William Mercer told everyone he owned the house and property. Nobody questioned it. You need to consider back then out here in the middle of nowhere, nobody thought to question the legality of ownership, even when there was no evidence of a legal or handwritten will when it came to a grieving widow. In addition, David took it upon himself to secretly put money into her bank account, which allowed Sharon to live comfortably for the remainder of her life should she chose not to remarry. He threatened to have her evicted and take away the money if she and her cronies did not stop spreading rumors. Sharon led him to believe she agreed to his demand, but as we all learned, she was not about to agree. Instead, she tried to kill both you and the rest of us. Instead, she ended up destroying three houses and killing five innocent people. I hope that answers your question about the deal he had with Sharon. Now it's my turn to ask a question. Why are you hesitating to marry David? It is obvious to everyone you love each other, apparently to everyone but you."

Cindy covered her face with her hands and began to cry again. Between sobs she managed to tell John she did love and want to marry David.

"What are you waiting for?" he asked. "The man is head over heels in love with you! He has overcome loss and PTSD, so pick up your phone and make the call! Tell him you love and want to marry him right now! Use my phone. I've already dialed his number."

David's cell phone rang twice before the litany of reasons why he should not pick up went through his mind. David tapped the option to communicate he was driving and could not take the call.

"At least I tried," sighed John. "When he returns what he thinks is my call I will tell him it is important that he call you right away."

Jake opened and stuck his head inside the screen door. "What is going on in here? The burgers are going to be burnt if the two of you don't come back out to the patio to eat, and don't forget the potato salad. We are starving out here!" John moved behind Cindy out of her line of sight. He motioned for Jake to keep quiet by placing a finger over his mouth. Jake got the message and stepped back outside, closing the screen door.

"Be out in a minute," offered Cindy. "I got something in my eye and John removed it." She knew it was a lie, but it was the best response she could think of at the time besides agreeing it was time to eat. She hurried unsteadily to the refrigerator to get the potato salad. Jake gave a questioning look at John through the screen. "Not now," John mouthed as the three of them trouped back to the patio to join the others, John holding Cindy's arm to support her.

Two days passed before David returned John's call. "Hey buddy, where in the hell have you been?" questioned John.

"I'm at the farm in Kansas. Why do you want to know?" replied David.

"You are where?" asked John. When David repeated his response, John groaned. "Why didn't you have the courtesy to let any of us know you were leaving?"

"We are all gown men. I don't have to report to any of you what I choose to do," replied David curtly.

"Did you forget you are in charge of overseeing the welfare of six other ex-military personnel, in addition to one lovely lady who happens to love you?"

"I advised the VA I was no longer in charge of the house or any of you, and they needed to get off their backsides and find someone else. As for Cindy, I was whistling Dixie in the dark when I thought she might love me!" came his heated response before excusing himself. "Someone is knocking at the door. Goodbye."

Dejected by the response of the person he believed to be a friend, John snapped his cell phone shut, but not before trying to contact Cindy with the latest news. He got the same automated response. Cindy also hit the one revealing she was driving and would get back to the caller. "Why is everyone suddenly on the road driving? Whatever happened to staying connected with people you believe are friends?" mumbled John.

CHAPTER THIRTY-ONE

Knocking persisted on David's door. *One of these days I need to put a peep hole in that door*, thought David in response to the knocking. "Who is it?" he asked as he approached the door to the Kansas farmhouse entryway.

"Open the door and find out," said a familiar female voice.

Oh my God, that can't be Cindy! She is in Oregon. Then again, I hope that isn't my ex-wife! "Just . . . just a minute," he mumbled before opening the door wide enough to see Cindy standing there with a tentative smile and a suitcase in her hand.

"You don't happen to have any extra food and a guest room for a weary traveler, do you?" she asked. "I have been driving practically non-stop for two days to get here. I'm tired and hungry."

Stunned by her unexpected appearance, he motioned her inside before he could ask what brought her to Kansas. Cindy entered and set her suitcase on the floor ahead of her before continuing, "Once upon a time in a land far, far away by the name of Riverwood, Oregon, I met a drifter," she began. "The drifter and I became friends. That led to him falling in love with me and asking me to marry him. He didn't hang around long enough for my answer. So, I decided to follow him to the land known as Kansas to let him know I do love him and want to be his wife."

Two seconds later she felt his arms around her, their lips meeting in a passionate kiss. It was David's turn to cry. "Forgive me. I was a fool to walk away without letting anyone know I was leaving. When I thought you didn't love or want to marry me, I didn't want to continue living in Oregon. In a mental fog, I gathered up a few clothes and drove here, thinking this is where I would live alone until I die."

"You will not be living or dying alone unless you tell me to leave," said Cindy.

"But you have a life and a lot of money waiting for you in Oregon," countered David.

"I signed everything in Melvin's will over to the city with the stipulation they turn my house into a home for military personnel suffering from PTSD. I authorized some of the money, the twenty-five thousand dollars I am entitled, to be redirected. The town council accepted my proposal to build separate quarters for female military personnel. Men aren't the only ones who deal with PTSD."

"That means you gave up everything for me?" questioned David.

"Not everything. I have money tucked away for a rainy day left from Harold's pension and life insurance policy, and

I will receive a stipend from the government for the use of my house and land," she replied while looking intently into his eyes. "I am good at gardening. I hear Kansas has fertile soil, so at least we won't starve if the offer to be your wife still stands."

"Only if you promise to bake one of those chocolate cakes no less than every week," teased David.

"I will bake one every day, if you like," she replied.

"Not unless you want a fat husband," came his answer.

"Fat, skinny, tall, short, I will love you no matter where life leads us."

"By the way, how did you learn I was here at the farm?" questioned David.

Did you forget cell phones show where a call originates, or I just might have extrasensory powers that lock in on the location of drifters like a homing pigeon? Especially when it comes to a man by the name of a David Mercer who happens to live on a farm in Kansas?"

"I must have told you the farm's location when I was out of my mind in the hospital," insisted David.

"I will never tell," she replied with a laugh and another heartfelt embrace and kiss.

Cindy did not spend the night or any other nights in David's guest room. They were married six weeks later, which was the time it took Oregon friends to form a caravan to make the trip from Riverwood to the Kansas Grange Hall large enough to accommodate them and the locals who would attend their wedding.

Ten months later Cindy presented David with a bouncing baby boy. Six months after the birth, they were guests of David's buddies who continue to live in the Riverwood house Cindy and Harold built. The men got acquainted with the baby. David decided to keep the Victorian house once occupied by his parents then Sharon, but insisted it be redecorated to Cindy's taste to be used as their summer retreat and future retirement home.

It did seem odd during their Oregon visits not to hear rumors about them with Sharon Murphy out of the picture. Her three demands for a retrial were all denied. Out of money, and given the fact no reputable attorney would take her case any further, made it clear Sharon would serve the rest of her life in prison where she belonged. Apparently, her life sentence served as a reminder of what could happen whenever anyone in Riverwood got the urge to start what could become a deadly rumor.

About the Author

Linda Ellen (Petty) Lynch was born on a small farm in Franklin County, Ohio. She is a retired registered nurse and business owner. She now resides in Southern California.

Other books by Linda Ellen Lynch
Secrets on Sand Beach
Blood
Emerald Valley
What the Heart Wants
A Time to Move On